BREAKING PATHS

Stories of Women Who Dared

MEERA KHANNA

olive turtle

NIYOGI BOOKS

Published by
NIYOGI BOOKS
Block D, Building No. 77,
Okhla Industrial Area, Phase-I,
New Delhi-110 020, INDIA
Tel: 91-11-26816301, 26818960
Email: niyogibooks@gmail.com
Website: www.niyogibooksindia.com

Editor: Mohua Mitra
Design: Shashi Bhushan Prasad/Cover: Mistunee Chowdhury

ISBN: 978-93-89136-00-5
Publication: 2019

Printed at: Niyogi Offset Pvt. Ltd., New Delhi, India

"However long the night, the dawn will break."
African Proverb

To the amazing spirit of women,
who in the darkness, find their dawn

Contents

Preface

Do women need to navigate spaces?

Often the personifying adjectives used for the traditional women in India and Pakistan are 'adjusting and accommodating.' Through centuries, by means of traditions, legends, myths, superstitions proverbs, folk lore, role models and advice given by mothers to daughters, the pressure on women to conform has been strong and consistent, insidious and deadly in its motivational indoctrination.

These are the stories of eighteen strong women who daily fight the suffocation of conformity. These are the stories of winners. These are not winners in the conventional sense of the word, in the sense they don't instigate a revolution or make a difference to the social milieu. But these are fighters of their circumstances, brave in their refusal to accept conventional limitations, determined in their decision to carve their futures, and courageous in their acceptance of the consequences. For them every day is a challenge; for everyday relationships and expectations conspire to erode their dignity and identity. Every day the space in their homes, hearts, souls and bodies is being encroached upon. Yet rooted in their cultural milieu, they make their choices, fight for it and succeed, all within the social framework. That perhaps is their greatest strength. They don't destroy existing frameworks because their identities don't fit within it. Within those constraining frameworks they, for a moment or for lifetime, take control of their lives

Within the given parameters they strategise to make space for themselves. That speaks volumes for their courage.

Guess Who Came to Dinner?

Safina Begum

Safina Begum pushed her young daughter up the rickety wooden stairs into the attic, amidst the over ripe apples. She looked at the leering armed figure in front of her and said briskly, "If you as much as look at my daughter, I will scream that a militant has taken shelter in my house. The *faujis* are only waiting to take shots at militants." The thickly bearded figure looked at her and smiled lecherously, "Begum, after I am killed, you think the *faujis* are going to leave your daughter? Better that she pleases a Mussalman than a kafir." Safina spat out, "Once you are dead, we'll be free of you. We will handle the soldiers ourselves. But get this into you head, you touch my children, and I'll harm you. You have forced yourself into my house. I am caught between the soldiers' guns and yours. But don't push my fear too far."

"All right, all right Begum. Give me food and shelter for tonight and tomorrow I'll be gone."

Safina stirred the rice in the pot, all the time keeping a sharp eye on the militant. It was obvious he was not a Kashmiri. But he seemed to know the village well, since he had chosen her house to take refuge from the chasing security forces. There was no male member in her house. Safina's husband had died of stomach cancer a year ago. Her two boys were too small to be of any consequence. Her house stood at a little distance from the village and the backyard opened out into thick wooded land. Safina shuddered as she thought of that morning, when at first light, she had opened the door to gather firewood. This huge mufflered figure had bounded in from the forest, pushed her in and shut the door. He had threatened to kill her two boys, if she made the slightest noise. And he meant business. When Bahadur had barked persistently at the unwelcome guest, the militant had shot him dead with his silencer fitted gun. Safina's eyes filled with tears as she remembered Bahadur trotting behind her as she collected dried pine cones from the forest. Her heart had wrung when she saw her children blubbering in grief, only to be frightened into a desperate silence.

Tension was palpable in the house as she served the unwelcome guest freshly cooked rice and kahwa. The children sitting on their beds watched the militant guzzling the food in haste. Safina thought that a whole day had to pass before the terror left her home...if he left. Nobody could leave the house till then and nobody could come in. The militant sat near a peep hole to keep watch on the searching soldiers. Throughout the day, the soldiers were moving in and out of the forest, searching for the militant. But they had not started a "cordon and search" operation of the village as yet, as their informers had not given them any clue on militants hiding in the village. Safina was sick with apprehension. She knew it was only a matter of time before the soldiers started searching each house in the village. She thought, this devil will get killed but he will kill everyone else in the bargain. For sheltering a terrorist Safina and her children were not likely to be shown any mercy. Grim thoughts chased each other in Safina's mind;

my flower like girl…how many times will she be raped before getting a reprieve in death? My boys, what bestiality will they have to suffer? I will be tortured, imprisoned and convicted, if I am not killed outright. Safina had never felt so helpless before, not even when her husband had died leaving her with three children.

†

The day dragged on slowly. Safina went about her chores with the militant watching her grimly. Safina sent her sons to keep their sister company in the attic. Tension mingled with fear and dread weighed down Safina's heart. Somehow, before the soldiers start their search operation, I have to get this brute out of the house. But how? The *azaan* resounded through the village calling the faithful to the evening prayer. From the window Safina saw the soldiers going off, as they did not want to disturb the *namaz*. But they are sure to start searching tomorrow, thought Safina. The militant thought so too. He laughed menacingly, "I will stay till I get a message from my comrades or till the soldiers come. Then we will die together in the gun fire." Safina felt sick. "I can't let my children go to certain death like this. I have to do something," she thought to herself.

She got up and called her daughter downstairs. Turning to the militant she said, "I am going to the edge of the forest to collect some mushrooms for dinner as there is nothing to eat in the house. I am leaving my sons behind, so you can be sure I'll come back. I am not likely to inform anybody, since my sons are at the mercy of your gun."

The militant looked at her suspiciously. Hunger was tormenting him again. He came from across the border where they ate a full meal with *roti*s and meat dishes, not rice with bits of meat thrown in. At least mushrooms will taste like meat, he thought.

Safina went out and took care to pluck poisonous toadstools, much to her daughter's astonishment. The bits and pieces of information that Safina had gleaned from her grandmother now came into use. Safina warned her daughter that they were not to eat the toadstool curry. This is my last chance, she thought. These toadstools will either kill him or at least make him so ill that he will be helpless. At home she warned the children not to come down from the attic. If the plan went awry, they were to jump from the attic on to the roof and run towards the village. Safina's hands shook as she pounded the spices for the curry. At last, after a hurriedly said prayer, she laid the rice and curry in front of the militant. He looked at her—

"Call one of your children to taste this dish."

Safina was prepared for this. "They break into rashes and get stomach cramps when they eat mushrooms. Then I'll have to call the village doctor. I will eat it in front of you." Safina took a piece from the dish and put it into her mouth. She pushed the morsel into her cheek, pretended to chew and swallow it.

"All right", growled the militant, hunger getting the better of his caution. With bated breath, Safina watched him eat, quietly replenishing his plate. Slowly she watched him slip into a helpless stupor. Thank God that the militant being an urban fellow had no clue of the vital difference between mushrooms and some of the wild poisonous toadstools.

†

Late at night, with the help of her elder son, Safina wrapped the militant in a blanket and dragged him to the forest. They kept a sharp lookout for the soldiers. Deep in the dark forest, she unwrapped the body. From her pheran, Safina took out her meat knife. For a moment she looked at the unconscious figure. She remembered the terror on her children's faces and the leering bestiality on the guest's face. She struck his chest with the knife pushing it in with all her might. Dead men would tell no tales, nor could they take revenge. She wiped the knife with the dried pine leaves and hurried her son back home. In the flickering light, she impressed on her children, the vital need to bury that day's events in the deepest recesses of their minds, never to be exhumed.

Morning brought great excitement to the village. The soldiers had through a well-planned ambush killed a dangerously armed militant in the forest. Posse of soldiers were milling through the forest. Photographs were clicked and all ammunition taken into custody. The officer in charge was already constructing in his mind the report that he was to send to the Corps Headquarters, the ambush, the chase, the overpowering odds and the final hand to hand fight in which a knife was used to kill the militant. What kind of a knife? What kind of a knife? Perhaps a khukri which soldiers often carried with them. One more 'kill' to the regiment's credit. One more commendation for the soldiers and officers.

Through the window, Safina watched the soldiers carry the body of the militant. Her children were safe…for now.

Strangers in my Home

Phoola

Phoola looked across the stream at her house that she could never enter. The stream gurgled merrily as if mocking her agony. A relentless agony that had begun one ghastly night in 1947 when raiders from Pakistan ran wild through parts of Kashmir, looting plundering and raping. Phoola, her husband and three children just managed to escape the *kabali*s who were targeting Hindu families. They crossed the stream and with that they crossed over one part of their lives. The Indian soldiers chased the raiders back, but irrevocable lines had been made in the lives of the people. The land across the stream remained with Pakistan as Pakistan Occupied Kashmir. Phoola lost everything to POK, her house, her belongings, her husband's small but prosperous shop. She lost her status as a businessman's wife and was reduced to eking out a living by cooking and washing in people's homes in the village of Salotri in Poonch district of Jammu and Kashmir. Her husband did odd jobs and hired himself out as a daily wage labourer. With desperate hard work, she and her husband managed to get a small house for the family. But it was just a house. Home was across the stream.

Every morning Phoola looked across at her home. She could see the smoke curling from her kitchen. What was being cooked on her hearth? Rotis for the children or was milk being boiled as she used to do every morning? She could see the mango tree on which her children had swung in gay abandon. But her beautiful courtyard which she swept clean every morning was a stable for the two horses. *Chhi!* The strong smell from the horses would enter her home. Phoola knew that her house was occupied by a Muslim family. The man seemed to be making a living by plying his two *tongas*. The house was always humming with activity as five children played, fought, ate and slept in Phoola's home. Phoola existed this side of the stream but lived across in her old home. She knew when the lanterns would be lit and which window was coming off its hinges. She watched as the woman in her home sat in the courtyard to clean the rice or cut vegetables. Phoola knew when her small vegetable patch yielded brinjals and when the season was for radish. She knew that the woman of the house had been washing, when she saw the rope between the trees weighed down by the clothes of seven people.

Some days Phoola resented the intrusion of her home, and the loss of a known way of life. The loss would have been more bearable, if her husband had found a more respectable job. Having sat in the shop all day, his bones had turned soft and now they creaked as he bent double under the weight of bags of rice or flour. Phoola, used to being her own mistress for most of her married life, found being at the beck and call of others irksome. But that was life, she conceded. They did not lose everything because she was a spendthrift or because her husband was a gambler. We lost all due to *kismet* and who can change that?

Gulabo looked across the steam at the woman on the other side looking at her silently as always. It was eerie, thought Gulabo. Whenever I look that side the woman's eyes are boring into me like some kind of a *bhoot.* When Gulabo woke up in the morning and washed her hands and face, the woman would be sitting on her doorstep looking her way. Gulabo washed clothes, cut vegetables cleaned the horse stable all under the eyes of the woman. It was like having a mother-in-law staring hard to find faults, thought Gulabo wryly. She wished she could unravel the mystery of the staring woman. Gulabo was new to the village of Teetrinot in Pakistan Occupied Kashmir. In the wake of the war between India and Pakistan, Gulabo and her family had left Rawalakote and settled here in Teetrinot. Most of the inhabitants of the village were outsiders, who had very little clue about the original people of the village. But Gulabo knew that the house belonged to a house proud woman. When they had shifted in after paying money to the *lambardar* of the village, Gulabo had found the house spick and span. The brass vessels in the kitchen gleamed like gold. The grain bin was overflowing and all the jars were full to the brim with mango, lime and vegetable pickles. The garden patch was replete with winter vegetables and small designs decorated every door and window. Gulabo mused on her good luck in getting a good deal with the house. Her husband was a hard-working man, a little short tempered, but otherwise caring.

She went out in the fading afternoon sun to clean the vegetables for the evening meal. As she sat down in her courtyard, by force of habit she looked across the stream and saw the woman again on the other side studying her carefully. Really, thought Gulabo, I must find out who she is and why she is so interested in me. But how? She could shout across the stream but her voice would be drowned by the noisy gurgling of the waters. And worse, the Pakistani Rangers would hear her and take her away for questioning. Their outpost was nearby and from their tower they kept a watch on all the activities on both sides of the Line of Control. She could see the Indian outpost too. Soldiers on both sides controlled the lives of the villagers of Salotri and Teetrinot, forcing them to live within the constraints of political wrangling of the two governments. Gulabo did not understand all this. But she knew that she had to steer clear of the soldiers from both sides. Her husband had dinned it into her and the children's heads.

But Gulabo was obsessed with the mystery of the staring woman. It rankled her all day. Phoola was obsessed with her previous home. She could never let go of her past. That rankled her all day.

†

Phoola tossed on the hard floor, as she heard her husband snoring loudly after a hard day's back-breaking work. He never mentioned their old home. It was as if he obliterated it completely from his memory, in the worry for the future. The children lived in the present, with the ups and downs of their little lives. It was only Phoola who clung to the past, unable to let go of past identities. She hardly had any friends in the village. Most of the women at the village well saw her as a 'haughty piece'. But Phoola caught in the nostalgia of the past and the immediacy of the present, always felt disoriented. She rose to drink a glass of water in an earthen glass. She remembered the set of twelve shining brass glasses that she had brought with her from her parents' home at the time of her marriage.

Her breath smelt strongly, a reminder of her meagre meal of *chapattis* and raw onions. There was never enough pulses or vegetables to satiate everyone's appetite. After many months Phoola railed silently against her fate. It was as if the numbness of the shock of relocation had worn off and she could feel every emotion clearly. She resented this hand-to-mouth existence, the perpetual worn-out face of her husband and the shabby clothes of her children. She resented this bare meal of dry *chapattis* and one dal without any rice or vegetable or chutney or curd.

Phoola sat on her doorstep and for the first time faced a fact that she had never breathed to anyone, not even her husband. All through the months of trauma, she had avoided thinking of it since the enormity of the loss would swamp her. In the days of prosperity, Phoola had saved from the housekeeping money her husband gave her. Small coins, a rupee from the money given by her brothers at Rakhi, a little bit from selling some vegetables. Slowly she had saved three thousand rupees which she had put in a ceramic jar and buried under the mango tree. When they left in a hurry at night, fearing the raiders, Phoola only had time to gather her children. She had never dared to mention this loss to her husband. He had never known that she had saved the money, so why give him pain on something that he was unaware of, reasoned Phoola. But all that wealth was there under the tree, while they lived like beggars. Resentment filled Phoola with bitterness. Now that Mussalman family will unearth and enjoy my money. God was truly blind and deaf and dumb. Could he not see their misery? Maybe they would never find the money. Why would they dig the ground for no reason? What use is that wealth to anyone under the ground? If it is of no use to me, it is better if it just rots under the tree. Could she go over one night and get the money out? The thought was squashed as soon as it rose. Meher Singh who had followed his wandering sheep to the other side had not come back still. God alone knows whether he is alive or dead? If I fall into the hands of the Mussalman or the Pakistani soldiers my fate will be worse than death. Besides that family might just take the money away and keep it for themselves. After all it is their home now. But the money is mine.

The persistent thoughts kept Phoola awake all night. For days Phoola's thoughts kept harking back to the jar of money. She kept working out schemes to get the money back, and rejected each plan, since it was foolhardy. Every time she looked at her house across the stream, she could only see the jar of money. The knowledge of the hidden wealth only agonised her. Gulabo on the other hand went about her days in blissful oblivion, even though the wealth was just a few feet away.

One evening Phoola was sitting near the stream when she heard wailing from across. *Hai Rabba*, what misfortune has fallen on my home? She could see the man of the house being brought in by other men. It was obvious he had been hurt and was writhing in pain. Phoola strained to see clearly, through the big crowd in the courtyard. All evening Phoola was beset with doubts and worry for a family of whom she knew nothing and with whom she had no connection. Phoola could not get through her chores the next day. She had no clue as to what had happened, but she knew a pall of gloom had settled on her home. From this side of the stream, she could feel the burden of sorrow. She could see that in the courtyard of the house there was only one horse and tonga. The other seemed to be missing. A couple of weeks later, Phoola's heart skipped a beat when she saw the woman helping her husband to a charpoy in the courtyard. He had lost one hand and a leg. He was limping painfully as he sat down leaning on his wife. Phoola's eyes welled with tears at the thought of the misfortune that had befallen her home. She wanted to reach out in sympathy. But how?

†

Gulabo sat on the edge of the stream, listlessly sorting out the clothes to be washed. Her back was breaking, less with physical exertion and more due to the uncertain future looming ahead. Her husband was incapable of driving a *tonga* again. Their beloved Shera had been killed when the brakes of the bus failed and it crashed into the waiting tonga. Thank God that her husband had been saved. But saved for what? According to him Allah had saved him for a fate worse than death. Incapable of earning for his family, he was destined to see his children and wife slowly starve to death. How long could they survive on the generosity of neighbours and the mosque? Already neighbours had started hinting that he sell the house at a distress price so that they could eat for some time. Who would hire a one armed and one legged labourer? Gulabo felt the tears coursing down her cheeks, when she thought of the disappointed faces of her children as they left for school after a frugal meal of *chapatti* and green chillis with salt. The income from one *tonga* was just keeping them on the borderline of starvation. Sulaiman, who was hired to drive the other tonga was daily reducing the income. He had millions of excuses. People paid less. They preferred to take the motor bus. Gulabo knew that he was taking advantage of their helplessness and cheating them of their money. She knew it was a matter of time before they would sell off the second tonga and Veera their beloved horse. With Shera gone, Veerá too was in the dumps. How long would that money keep seven people fed? What about medicines for her weak husband? Her gold loops had paid for it till now. But for how long?

Helpless, Gulabo slumped near the stream. Through her tears she could see the woman across the stream looking at her. The woman was shaking her head and wiping tears from her face. Gulabo sat up. What was she saying? She saw the woman point upwards as if to say Allah would take care. Gulabo did not know what to say or do! So she joined her hands in a *namaste.* Quickly she got up as she heard her husband's irritable voice calling for her.

Phoola was desperate to talk to the woman in her home. Next morning, she waded determinedly to the middle of the stream and deliberately started washing clothes on the big flat rocks there. From the corner of her eyes she could see the soldiers observing her. Phoola continued this for some days till she understood that the soldiers were no longer observing her. From the middle of the stream, if she was cautious, she could talk to the opposite bank without evoking suspicion. She waited for the woman to come to the bank of the stream. She did with a bundle of clothes. Phoola in between beating clothes on the rock attempted to talk to her.

"Your house was my home before the war," was her opening line. Gulabo felt elated at having the mystery solved.

"Oh! That is why you always look this side"

"Yes, we had happy times in that home. It is a blessed home."

Gulabo, in between soaping the clothes, kept a sharp eye on the observation post.

"We were also very happy, but now..." Gulabo's voice broke.

"What has happened to your husband?" Phoola asked.

Gulabo was relieved to pour out her woes to the strange woman from another nation. She felt that she was no stranger. Perhaps it was because they, by strange quirk of fate shared a home. Phoola quietly heard the misfortune that had swept this happy family in her home. All too soon it was time to go back to their chores, but not before they had fixed a common time for the next day.

For a few days Phoola and Gulabo's conversations continued. The soldiers soon came to see them as part of the landscape. Phoola eagerly asked about her house. Was the well full of water? It had the sweetest water in the whole village. The window of the big room would never shut properly. What were the vegetables growing in the little patch? Gulabo learnt of the ill wind that had swept Kashmir with the looting of the raiders. She heard of Phoola's climb down in social status and the struggles to keep starvation at bay. The theme was familiar and each woman reached out to the other, across the stream, washing off all borders and boundaries.

Fate was soon catching up with Gulabo. Phoola and her husband were working and somehow they were able to manage two square meals for their children. But starvation was facing Gulabo squarely in the face. The other horse and tonga had been sold to buy tonics for her husband. That money had warded off total misery for some time. Only that morning, Gulabo had discovered a small bottle of rat poison near her husband's bed. Cold fear gripped her, as she railed and ranted at him. He had no answer for her hysterical questions. Without his protective presence in the house, what was her status? She would have to finally sell herself to keep the children fed or like her husband, contemplate the easy way out. She poured out her misery to Phoola that day and cried bitterly at a fate which she could not avoid. Phoola heard her in silence while her heart bled for Gulabo and her home. That night Phoola kept hearing Gulabo's piteous voice. Was this the fate of her home, to be swamped in misery?

†

The morning saw Phoola washing clothes again on the rock in midstream. She asked Gulabo to meet her half a mile downstream. There the stream curved in such a way that the banks were very close to each other. Also the thick undergrowth made detection from any point impossible. Gulabo was intrigued. She tried to probe, but Phoola only impressed upon her the urgency to meet. That afternoon while her husband was asleep and the children playing, Gulabo took a bundle of firewood on her head. She needed an excuse for wandering about in the afternoon. Phoola pretended to look for the wild spinach that grew on the banks of the stream. But both kept the other in sight till they reached the spot. Gulabo crossed over and quickly both of then hid in the undergrowth. For the first time they saw each other closely, even though they had shared their closest thoughts. Spontaneously both hugged each other and smiled through the tears. Gulabo marvelled at her own courage in coming to the 'enemy' territory at the request of a stranger. But Phoola was no stranger.

Quickly Phoola explained her mission. "Listen *Behen*, there is one way by which all you troubles can be ended. Underneath the mango tree, five steps towards the left, I had buried a jar of money. I hope it is still there. Take it and use it to treat your husband and find him an occupation. Use it to buy grain and pulses."

Gulabo listened in astonishment. Were her ears deceiving her? Before she could probe further, they heard the sound of the buffaloes being driven towards the village. Phoola pushed Gulabo across the stream and pretended to dig the ground for spinach. A load had rolled off her and she was relieved. But the strange part was that she was not to get the money. Yet she was happy and at peace with herself.

Gulabo's thoughts were in a whirl. Was it true? If it wasn't, why would Phoola call her across despite the dangers? Was this the end of their troubles? Was this Allah's way of answering her prayers? Or was there some trick hidden in it? No, Phoola could not betray her. Inexplicably, Gulabo knew she could trust Phoola.

That night Gulabo waited impatiently for all to go to bed. Quietly, she dug the place and took out the jar. Her hands were shaking as she counted the money. Full 3000 rupees! Allah! This was a stroke of luck beyond her imagination.

Gulabo marvelled at Phoola's generosity. How hard she must have worked to save this money. With this money she could buy medicines, food, a buffalo, some means of livelihood for her husband. God, Thank you for this grace. Next morning, she was first at the stream. Quickly she told Phoola to meet her at the same spot in the afternoon. Phoola was eager to know whether she had found the money. Gulabo insisted that she would answer all queries in the afternoon. She pretended to fill her jar with water and ran home. Phoola was intrigued. Had anything gone wrong? Did the police get to know about the money? *Hai Rabba,* had she pushed Gulabo unwittingly into a new mess?

That afternoon, Gulabo quickly made her way to the spot, full of impatience. She had tied the money to her salwar and it was hitting her thighs as she walked and half ran to the spot near the stream. As soon as Phoola came, Gulabo took out a bag of money and put into Phoola's hands.

"Behen, this is your money. Take it."

Phoola stood as if struck. "But Gulabo this money I wanted you to have."

"I have kept some money for myself too. This bag contains 1500 rupees and this one also contains 1500 rupees. I have divided the money equally. Believe me if it wasn't for my condition, I wouldn't have kept even this amount. But I could not have deprived you of your savings. Allah will never forgive me if I let your children starve." Phoola could not believe her ears. It was a moment too deep for words. They held each other's hands and communicated through their tears.

†

Phoola bought a buffalo and set up a small shop for her husband. So did Gulabo. The two women living across the borders shared their precious resources and managed a livelihood for their families. Phoola still looks at her old house and smiles with satisfaction at the laughter of children on both sides of the stream.

Harried Annapoorna

Pushpa Rani

Pushpa polished the tomato lovingly and balanced it on the pile. She flicked a duster on the potato pile, touched the glistening bell peppers and sprinkled water on the emerald green coriander. She liked to put the carrots next to the green chillies, the brown potatoes next to the pink onions, and the red tomatoes balanced below the white radishes. The contrasts coloured her drab life, weighing the vegetables and counting in the coins. Weigh, count. Weigh and count. The motion went on and on, relieved only by the vegetables; the tomatoes that tumbled into, and the potatoes that rolled onto the weighing pan. The onions sat heavily while the lotus stems stood erect. Pushpa wished that her customers would admire the colours, the texture and the inherent character of her vegetables. But they were always in a desperate hurry; women rushing back home from work, mentally planning easy menus while selecting the vegetables; distracted and harassed mothers leaving mischievous children behind; vacillating men torn between their favourite vegetables and their wives' firm orders.

At the juncture of two steep climbs in Mallital, in Nainital, was Pushpa's little vegetable shop. Her market savvy husband Gulab Singh selected this spot. At the end of a long panting climb, people stopped to take breath and spotted the vegetable shop. Minds clicked, vegetables selected and purses opened. Gulab Singh had no MBA degree to tell him about situational positioning. But his innate shrewdness inherited from the hills, where survival was a daily challenge, gave Gulab Singh an uncanny sense as to what would sell and how. It was he who went to the wholesale vegetable market every morning before he opened his small tea and cigarette shop.

†

He began the day with tea and parathas that Pushpa sleepily made for him. She hated parathas. Oily creatures! When they sizzled on the griddle, it seemed they were mocking her. "No time Pushpa, you've no time," they seemed to be hissing at her. Every morning dawned a sense of guilt in Pushpa. She started her round of never ending chores—sweeping, cleaning, washing, settling, storing, feeding, shopping, grinding, ironing, collecting fuel and fodder…the round was endless. Her mind urging her onto the next chore, leaving her no time to think and prepare a meal for her family. Pushpa did not prepare a meal. She only cooked food. Parathas and tea in the morning; rice and dal prepared and kept for the children when back from school; at night after closing the shop, Pushpa with aching joints had just enough strength to cook potatoes with spices thrown in as an accompaniment to the rotis made in a tearing hurry before the children nodded off to sleep.

The gnawing sense of dissatisfaction gathered momentum when Pushpa went to her vegetable shop. Each vegetable she handled reminded her of the dish that she could lovingly prepare.

The red tomatoes could be ground into a lip smacking chutney along with garlic and green chillies. Pushpa looked at the purple succulent eggplants and thought of the *bharta* that she had set out to make a few days back. Just as she was roasting the eggplants on the red hot coals, turning them at intervals, she had to rush to milk the lowing cow whose udders were overflowing. The cow was milked but the eggplants were charred. Nothing could be planned. No preparation carefully made, enjoyed and then presented. Rush, hurry and get on. That summed up her life.

Pushpa sighed and looked up. Champa Rani was trundling along to the shop, her stick tap tapping the cobbled stones. She was a difficult customer and a parsimonious one.

'Pushpa, what rotten vegetables have you got today?' grunted Champa, her grey hair glistening in the Himalayan sun.

"Amma, however rotten the vegetable, you will still make a feast out of it." Pushpa answered.

"Go on, you sweet-tongued woman. Don't think you can get a single rupee extra with all that sweet talk," said Champa Rani, smiling and taking the sting out of the words. She selected and rejected, picked up and dropped back. "My daughter-in-law excels in ruining every single vegetable. I don't know who taught her cooking, if she has been taught at all. Look at this okra. Can anyone ruin this excellent vegetable? But no. She'll make a mess out of even this."

Pushpa suggested slyly, "Amma, why don't you buy these okras and show her your culinary skill?" Champa fell into the flattering trap. She bought okras, onions, some bitter gourd and colocassia for good measure. She was in a hurry to show off to her daughter-in-law, so she didn't haggle too much.

Left alone, Pushpa dreamt of an okra preparation. Wash, dry and slit open the okra. Powder cumin, red chillies, rock salt and a pinch of asafoetida. Then stuff each okra, slowly filling every nook and corner. It would take time, but when the teeth bit into the juicy, spiced, fried okra then the taste was worth the time and effort.

"Pushpa, Pushpa, give me some eggplants"—a strident voice interrupted her reverie.

"Sorry Teacher ji, my thoughts were wandering. Eggplants? Here they are, juicy, no seeds, no worms, soft and tasty. Is Teacher Bhai going to get *bharta* today?"

"No way" answered the teacher. "I have 90 books to correct. I am just going to cut it up and toss it into the pan with some spices. Who has the time to roast them patiently?"

She stuffed them into her bag and swiftly walked away, ramrod straight.

Pushpa thought of her children in school, who would rush back home ravenous to eat rice and dal. She wished she had ground some onion chutney for them, instead of washing the bedclothes. But they were stinking, argued Pushpa defensively to herself. Today she would leave the shop early and make an okra preparation with the rotis. Having decided, Pushpa felt happy and got through the day—weighing and packing, persuading and cajoling, selling and earning. All the while she glanced at the okra she had carefully chosen and kept aside. That evening Pushpa was putting away the weighing scales when three women from the nearby houses strolled up to the shop. They chattered, gossiped, giggled while selecting the vegetables; in no hurry to go back home to the grind of cooking, serving and washing up. Pushpa gritted her teeth, trying hard not to let her impatience annoy her customers. Finally they left, leaving her richer by forty rupees and poorer by thirty minutes. She had just picked up her umbrella when Chhottu from the Sher-e-Punjab restaurant came to buy onions, garlic and tomatoes that they had run out of. Pushpa prayed to Devi that no other customer would come.

She rushed uphill, her knees trembling with haste. It was already quarter past eight, according to the church clock and she still had a half hour climb. Her children were sitting outside, dirty and dishevelled. Pushpa rushed in without pausing for breath, and put the bath water to heat. She washed her face and replenished the sindoor on her forehead, before lighting the lamp in front of her numerous pictured gods. She rushed around the house, putting away clothes, books and shoes. She swiftly spread the beds on the floor because her son was already nodding off to sleep. She put the hay for the cow, which looked at her in dumfounded gratitude.

Hardly had Pushpa washed the okras, when her daughter cried out, "Ma, I am hungry. Chintu has gone off to sleep. We did not have any milk in the evening as the pan overturned." Pushpa dropped the idea of stuffing each okra with spices. She just cut them up and put them in the pan with spices. She heard the rain tapping on the tin roof and rushed out to get in the dry clothes. A charring smell greeted her in the kitchen. The green okras were liberally spotted with black. The cook in Pushpa rebelled, but the mother in her gave the okras to the hungry sleepy children.

Gulab Singh just gobbled the burnt okras, mentally calculating the profit for the day after paying the rent and the money to keep the beat policeman happy.

He is oblivious to what he is eating, thought Pushpa, potatoes or okras. Why does he put up with these makeshift meals? Why does he eat with a blank expression? Why do I feel guilty all the time?

Thoughts jostled each other in Pushpa's mind as she washed the dishes. She went to bed with a vague sense of disquiet. It persisted even when Gulab Singh reached out to her. The days went by in frustrated swiftness. Life seemed one long chain of hurried meals, nothing to relieve the monotony of uphill and downhill; nothing to satisfy her craving to cook a good meal.

†

Pushpa stood at the electronics shop looking at the pictures of well-groomed women who cooked effortlessly and smiling all the time. She wondered how they kept their nails pink the entire time and why their sindoor did not stream down their foreheads with sweat. Her focus shifted to the other TV that was showing a feature on Kashmir. Tall pines, glistening lakes, grand mountain ranges. For her, brought up in the hills of Nainital, it was a familiar sight. Her eyes were riveted to the sight of a Kashmiri woman in a boat, selling flowers. What was that? Was she cooking in the boat as she rowed from customer to customer?

Pushpa's legs took her uphill while her mind clicked on endlessly. She had a single point agenda for the next few days. Every day after giving Gulab Singh all her earnings she asked for twenty rupees. He questioned her closely but on facing a stubborn silence, gave up. A day dawned when Pushpa woke up with a pleasant sense of anticipation. She checked and rechecked the bag that she had packed the night before. She finished her chores and watched the children going downhill to school, their sturdy legs making light of the dangerous slopes. As she opened the shop, Pushpa's heart was filled with many doubts. She quelled them as she lit the incense in front of the small altar in the shop. She placed in front of her shop the small charcoal stove that she had recently bought. She arranged the red-hot coals on it and carefully placed a succulent eggplant to roast. Her customers strolled in. Questions were asked, doubts raised, encouragement given and assurances made. All the while, Pushpa never lost track of the roasting eggplants. The aroma of the cooking *bharta* incited many to buy the eggplants that day. By evening Pushpa had managed to make a *bharta* and a tasty concoction of cauliflower, peas and tomatoes. She packed it all in the big lunch box that had been presented to her on her wedding day. She had never travelled or gone on picnics. Now at last the lunch box had come in use.

As she walked home that night, Pushpa reflected on her day. It had been a busy day, no time to stand and stare between customers. Any time snatched from her salesmanship was invested in cutting, chopping and frying. Her mind sang as she raced the last few steps home. She smiled mysteriously at her children as she swiftly settled the house. She could not take her eyes off her children as they ate. Satiated laughter filled the kitchen. Gulab Singh looked at her and smiled as he licked his fingers. Pushpa felt fulfilled.

Pushpa's little vegetable shop is an even more happening place. She sells fresh vegetables and cooked curries for the harassed housewives, busy teachers and the bachelors living down the road. It is hard work, the business of planning a three-course menu, the time management, the cutting and chopping, the cooking and tasting. She reaches home only in time to feed her sleepy children the three-course meal.

Sometimes all this seems too much for her. Pushpa shrugs. That is life. Always on the run.

Death Money

Maryam Begum

"Your husband was a militant," the cold pitiless voice resounded in the room. Maryam Begum clutched her application, unable to comprehend that this one line struck down her claim to widow's pension. "But Sahib, he is dead. I am a widow, how can I live without help?"

The cold voice became perceptibly colder—"Your husband was killed by security forces in an encounter. He is a militant."

Those with legitimate and illegitimate claims to the widows' pension pushed Maryam Begum aside. Was her husband a militant? Was he a militant because he carried a gun or because he went across the border to be trained in violence? Had he killed a soldier or anybody else? Who knows? Maryam Begum trudged on wearily up to the house perched precariously on a cliff…thoughts whirling in her mind. She looked at the four boys playing, oblivious that their future had been darkened. Maryam felt an impotent anger against their father. Son of a dog, made all the wrong decisions and got himself killed, leaving me with four big mouths to feed.' The land untilled, the grain store empty and not a single rupee in the house. Maryam Begum looked across the mountains and wept tears of frustration.

Having to maintain the façade of docile sorrow, when her soul shrieked at the injustice of her situation was Maryam's biggest curse.

The donkey could not even be a successful militant...she silently thundered at her own misfortune. Look at Shah Begum's husband, who last summer came across and gave her 30,000 rupees...she thought to herself in utter frustration. And she had to be saddled with this man who could only saddle her with more burdens...she fumed! In her widowhood, Maryam Begum could only see the lost futures of her sons. The daily grind of having to manage on nothing had washed away all affection, leaving only hardness and a fierce determination to give her sons a future.

Purposefully she rose and gave her sons salted tea and wild apples. Then she trudged up the mountain path to Ahmad Wani's house. She clearly remembered the number of times Ahmad Wani had come to her house trying to persuade her husband to take up the gun. Maryam Begum was fiercely determined to confront Ahmad Wani and make him pay for the consequences. Not finding him at home, she hid among the trees, confident that he would come furtively at night to see his newborn son. She was not wrong. In the flickering moonlight, under the creaking chinar trees she caught hold of him. Ahmad Wani, the gun-toting militant cowered under Maryam Begum's berating. He was speechless in the face of the raging mother. Bewildered as he was, he soon comprehended that Maryam Begum wanted compensation for her husband's death. He was aghast. Who would give her the compensation?

"Those agents of death for whom you and my husband work for..." declared Maryam Begum triumphantly. "After all they are sitting safe somewhere, while you people do the dirty work. If I can't get pension from the Sarkar, let me get it from the *jehadi*s!"

Ahmad Wani blubbered, and implored, helpless in the face of Maryam Begum's ire. Finally he consented to talk to the self-styled commander. She was still obstinate, for she had no faith in Ahmad Wani.

"I want to talk to your 'commander' myself," she declared much to Ahmad Wani's horror.

"Do you know what kind of men they are? They'll rape and kill you," blustered Ahmad Wani.

"What else can you men do? Rape kill, rape kill. That is your idea of *azadi,*" Maryam spat out in contempt.

†

Through the night, Maryam Begum stuck to him like a leech, alternately coaxing and abusing him. Finally cornered Ahmad Wani trudged through the dark jungles, through culverts and streams with Maryam Begum doggedly following him. It seemed an interminable journey for her. Sometimes she suspected that Ahmad Wani was purposely taking her through a circuitous route in the hope of shaking her off. But she did not flinch. Every time her feet cried out to her, her heart cried for her sons. Finally at dawn, Ahmad Wani reached a clearing in the thickly wooded forest. Having made Marayam wait in the shadows, he went ahead to meet the 'commander' of the business of death. Maryam peeped to see them gesticulating fiercely. At last unable to bear the suspense any longer, she stepped out. The men looked at her, astonished expressions soon giving way to lecherous glances.

Maryam Begum looked at the men and deliberately said in strident tones—"If I don't go back to my village with my body and honour intact, you'll not get a single man from the Dewarlolab area to do your dirty work. The whole village knows I've come here."

The death hardened men conferred in furtive whispers. Ahmad Wani, anxious not to create further trouble, exhorted them to pay some money to Maryam Begum to get her off their backs.

"How much?" barked the 'commander'.

"Four lakhs," replied Maryam calmly.

"Four lakhs! Was your husband an army officer?" The men sniggered.

"I only know my husband died doing your work. I have four sons. A lakh each for their future."

Ahmad Wani whispered something. The 'commander', impatient to be gone before he confronted the security forces tried to buy time.

"I don't have that much money with me. I need to get it from across. Meet me here after three days and I'll see what I can do."

Maryam laughed mirthlessly. "You think I'll trust you! I am coming with you. I don't care who gives me money. Somebody has to compensate me for my man's death."

The desperate men, who could outwit security forces, plan and execute ambushes, were at a loss with Maryam's cussedness. It would have been child's play to put a bullet through her.

But the 'commander' was wary of the consequences. It was becoming increasingly difficult to recruit Kashmiri men as *jehadis*. Dewarlolab was a fertile ground for recruitment. Too fertile to be lost for a couple of lakhs.

Once again, Maryam straggled behind the bearded taciturn men. Crawling under barbed wires, through ditches, skulking here and creeping there, she reached the terrorist training camp. She had no idea where she was, but she knew that this was not her homeland. Maryam was made to wait in the kitchen shed, tired, hungry, and weary but still determined. A woman silently handed her a glass of tea. Looking at each other there was a swift communion of sympathy, for lives caught irrevocably in the violent games men play. Looking through the smoke grimed kitchen window, Maryam saw young boys with guns aimed at olive green effigies of soldiers. If it wasn't for the guns resounding, they could be mistaken for playing boyish games of 'police and thieves'. For a moment Maryam had a ghastly vision of her young boys with grim faces handling these toys of destruction.

With the money she could perhaps take them away from the village and put them in a school far away from the *jehadis* and *fidayeens*, away from the talk of death and destruction, she mused hopefully. Maryam stayed in the camp for three whole days. Finally she was called to meet the self-styled divisional commander. Ahmad Wani was there obsequious and smirking. A packet was handed to her. "This contains two lakhs. We can't give more. Take it and get out."

Maryam, with swift fingers checked and packed the bulky bundle and tied it to her back. It was cumbersome but she was ensuring her sons' futures. She began the long trudge back with Ahmad Wani. They crossed the Line of Control, dodging searchlights and search parties. Wading through the stream stealthily, she could see Ahmad Wani in front of her. One minute he was there, next moment, he was slumped in the water. Before Maryam Begum could even react, she heard gunshots. She felt something hitting her. "Am I dead? Will I see my sons again?" Fear propelled her feet and she ran across the water into the dark woods. Zigzagging, she managed to give the ambush party the slip. Hiding and running, she managed to last the night.

†

When the day dawned, she realised that she was near a village close to her home. Evading curious eyes, she trudged back to her home, thankful that she was alive to see her sons. They were out playing. Sitting under the cherry tree, she opened her bundle. Whole bundles had been damaged by the bullets that had grazed by, leaving gaping burn holes. Not a single note was intact.

Tears rolled down incessantly as Maryam Begum looked at her children.

Needle in the Banana

Nalini

"Look at the state of this cupboard," with a hoot of derisive laughter Arun held open the door to reveal books stuffed together helter skelter. "What is the point of polishing the furniture when cupboards are in an utter mess?"

Nalini looked around at her newly renovated drawing room, the raw silk curtains, the upholstered sofas, the glinting crystal and the shining silver. She had spent hours in the shop looking, selecting and matching to finally get the result that she wanted, a tasteful subtly elegant drawing room, and the right background for a successful corporate ladder climber. Arun had very little time or inclination to do up the house. But he certainly had the inclination to pull her down, particularly in front of others.

Nalini turned hurt eyes towards her visitors and camouflaged it behind a sheepish smile, "Arun has such a wonky sense of humour." She could see the bewilderment on their faces, wondering why a man should deliberately point out an untidy cupboard in a spick and span room. It was almost as if he derived pleasure in focussing on the job not done in the face of millions of jobs done, and done well. Nalini had often been perplexed by this trait in Arun's nature. It wasn't as if he did not love her or care for her. He was a good husband in the sense he gave her immense freedom, never grudged her money and loved her in a rather careless fashion. If he did not actively encourage her in her activities, he did not discourage her either. Nalini worked hard at being a good home maker, a neat house, meals perfectly cooked and beautifully presented, guests well entertained and fed. Nalini worked harder at being a good wife. She gave 100 per cent of herself generously to Arun, loved him with a single minded focus and admired him greatly for his competence and determination to succeed in life.

On the face of it they seemed well matched. But a faint sense of disquiet troubled Nalini all the time. She could never fathom even after eight years of marriage, whether Arun was really pleased with any gesture or effort that she made. She often recalled a hot sweaty Sunday afternoon when she struggled in the kitchen to dish up a gourmet Chinese meal. At the table the only remark Arun made was, "The chicken is soggy."

Nalini had consoled herself by saying, "Perhaps he cannot express his appreciation." But her mind played the Devil's advocate in saying, "He can express his criticism vociferously enough."

It was not Arun's lack of appreciation that bothered Nalini. It was this strange, almost sadistic tendency in him to prick her confidence, to humiliate her if front of others; to take perceptible pleasure in her discomfort. Of course it was all done in the garb of good humour, but often Nalini wondered how any remark could be funny when it was calculated to hurt and hurt abominably. When she protested, she was made to feel like a kill joy who could not take a joke on herself. Nalini in her naivety took his hurtful remarks seriously and tried to better each time.

But the harder Nalini tried, the better each job was done, the more hurtful was Arun's remarks. With each remark Nalini retreated further into a hurt shell. But the frustration raged inside her like a volcano. Rage at the futility of the pin prick statements, fury at being taken for granted, in believing that she neither needed appreciation nor did the humiliation affect her. Slowly and insidiously Arun's derision started freezing Nalini. But it was an iced fire, a cold fury that masked the rage in being scorned. The fire had to rage; and it did.

†

It all started with an innocuous statement that Nalini read in a magazine.

"Most people who are destructively critical are really hiding their own inadequacies." The line kept on whirling in Nalini's mind till she was forced to sit down and analyse the situation. Did Arun really feel inadequate in front of her? Did he actually resent her competence, her grace and her capacity to achieve perfection in whatever she did? But what she did was so small compared to Arun's material and professional success.

That is the only role he fulfils. Everything else is taken care of by you Nalini, with minimum fuss and maximum efficiency, she reminded herself. Everyone recognised her competence, everyone except Arun. That perhaps was the reason for his sense of inadequacy. Nalini ruminated over these thoughts and counter thoughts for days. Yes, she did pack a lot of work into her day; running the home, taking care of the children's needs and education, keeping in touch with relations, entertaining friends, taking care of Arun's and her own parents, counselling continuously...all this while successfully running her small interior decoration business. Nalini reluctantly admitted to herself that perhaps Arun did suffer from a sense of inadequacy in the face of her capabilities.

Nonplussed, Nalini was at a loss to deal with the situation. Talking to Arun would only serve to embarrass him. Perhaps if she was to falter...For days Nalini faltered in her usual capability, made foolish mistakes or left jobs undone. Arun exploded even more, complained, cribbed and criticised. But he showed no inclination to shoulder any responsibility. His remarks became even more vicious and hurtful...till....

Nalini remembered that day well. It was a small party consisting of Arun's colleagues and their wives. Over drinks Arun was narrating a joke with the right inflections and pauses. After the laughter died down, Nalini looked at Arun and said, "That must be the tenth time I laughed at the same joke Arun. Even my acting is getting strained."

She turned to the others and said with a tinkling laugh, "Poor Arun, the monotony of his jokes is even funnier than his jokes."There was silence and then everyone started talking together to get over the moment. Arun looked at Nalini, bewildered and a wee bit hurt. His perplexity itself goaded Nalini on. Through the evening, she made snide remarks, all in the garb of good humour. With each remark, she was elated by the sense of power.

That was the first of many such evenings. Nalini perfected the art of sarcastic humour. Like most women she discovered that she could hurt and hurt abominably with her speech. But she was careful to introduce the right element of humour. Most of her remarks seemed downright funny, but they pricked Arun. It was like giving a needle in a banana. Only the one who consumed it knew where it pricked. Each time Nalini made remarks, Arun retreated further into a shell. In the beginning Arun retaliated with gusto, enjoying the sparring with words. But soon he realised that gentle, docile Nalini was not merely sparring. She was giving him a leveller and had no compunction in hitting below the belt. He was no match for her veiled derision and witty sarcasm. Her remarks levelled at him, evoked much laughter and much heartburn. But then... "Can't you take a joke?"

Slowly Arun stopped retaliating. He just maintained stoic silence. The façade of life went on. Nalini cared for him in a detached fashion. But she had tasted blood. She did not lose an opportunity to prick Arun. The pleasure was immense and addictive.

Talaq

Shabnam

Shabnam Begum stood in front of the Khap Panchayat of Saidpur village. Even in her subdued demeanour, the sex appeal that Shabnam oozed was unmistakable. Tension thickened the atmosphere as many men tried to look at her surreptitiously without their mothers or wives seeing the longing glances.

Shabnam stood in front of the caste Panchayat that was the grim police of the community morals. They decided who could love or rather lust whom; who was to be divorced and who to be ostracised. They were impartial, sombre and harsh enforcers of morality as they interpreted it. It was just accidental that most of their punishments and reprimands were reserved for the women. After all it was the woman who dragged man to sin; they, with their inviting looks and swaying hips that even the shapeless burka could not hide, enticed many to sin. The community would have strayed beyond redemption but for the Khap Panchayat.

It was they who decided that Ameena Begum should marry her brother-in-law after he raped her. Her divorced husband would henceforth be her brother. It did not matter to them, that Ameena loved her husband and hated her brother-in-law. The Khap had ordained that Bilkees would not marry the young Assistant Postmaster, Ali, but the aging Mohammad Khalid. Her parents had been forced to agree, fearful of being thrown out of the village. It was another matter that Mohammad Khalid fuelled by his desire for a young body had paid the Khap heavily for his lust.

Today the Khap had got together to judge the divorce of Shabnam Begum by Aslam. The reason for divorce was indeed grave—adultery. Aslam was accusing Shabnam of illicit relations with Moinuddin, the clerk at the sugar mill. "Shabnam has been unfaithful. I have already said *'talaq'* twice in the last two months. Now only one more utterance and I will be free of this bitch," growled Aslam.

Moinuddin was not present at the hearing. He had threatened to reject all the sugar cane of the Saidpur farmers if he was even mentioned in the Khap Panchayat. But the unspoken accusation hung heavy in the air. The Khap's work was cut out; pronounce the divorce and go back to the steaming biryani. Shabnam would go back to her village. Or would she?

The Panchayat elders shifted uneasily as they saw Shabnam standing unrepentantly straight. Even though she was modestly covered, the arrogance in her femininity was patently obvious. In the one year that she was married, she had created unprecedented havoc. Of course she cooked, cleaned and washed, but all with an air of nonchalance. She served Aslam demurely enough, but as if she was enjoying a private joke. Even when she faced Aslam's blows, she neither cried nor ranted, but bore all in silent disdain, which incensed Aslam even more. Something about Shabnam defied stereotyping. She did not quite fit in like the other burka clad women.

†

The Panchayat chief – the *mukhiya* – cleared his throat, hoping that the Maulvi would take control of the proceedings. But the Maulvi looked grimly ahead, weighed down by the tremendous weight of keeping community morals. "Shabnam Begum, your husband Aslam accuses you of adultery. This is a grave sin in the eyes of Allah. As such Aslam has full right to divorce you. Do you want to say anything?"

Shabnam Begum looked at each of the Panchayat members and then said deliberately, "Before this good-for-nothing pronounces the final *talaq,* ask him to place the *meher* amount and all my jewellery, here in front of everyone."

A gasp rippled through the crowd, as they heard this bold request. The Maulvi shifted his ponderous belly and said, "That is fair. To be free of Shabnam Begum, Aslam will have to give the *meher* amount."

Aslam looked helpless. This hearing was not going his way. He blustered and tried to wriggle out.

"I will pay the *meher* later. I don't want to keep a penny of this slut's money."

"Pay it now. If you can't, then the hearing will have to be called off", pronounced Ibrahim Ali, having finally got a chance to depress Aslam's pretensions above his station. Aslam could feel the sympathies of the crowd shifting. He felt that his manhood was at stake if he could not give the *meher* amount. He felt it increasingly vital to retain his arrogance in front of the Panchayat. But to give away Rs 15000, just like that! Aslam's mind was racing for options to get out without losing face.

He looked at Shabnam. Her eyes mocked him with a derisive twinkle. Aslam got up and swaggered to his house. He came back with the money wrapped in cloth along with Shabnam's meagre jewellery. He placed it in front of the Panchayat with a heavy heart. There went his dreams of owning another bullock.

The Panchayat was relieved. Now they could go back to their meal.

"Shabnam Begum, Aslam wants to divorce you, unable to bear your adulterous behaviour. Do you have anything to say?"

Shabnam looked at Aslam and then at each of the men sitting on the *chaupal*, waiting to degrade her and award the punishment. "Aslam should well know why I committed adultery, if I did."

A shock reverberated in the crowd echoing again and again through the hushed whispers. The Mukhiya felt with uneasiness that nothing would be the same again in the village.

"What do you mean" asked Aslam belligerently.

"What is a woman supposed to do if she is hungry and does not get food in her own house? She goes to the neighbour to satisfy the cravings of her body."

In the silence only the cawing of the crows could be heard, as if they were joining in Shabnam's contempt. Then a cacophony burst forth. A woman talking about her lust in front of the village elders. What was the world coming to? Some women looked at Shabnam with half concealed sympathy. A man's lust was his right and a woman's was her shame. Why?

"What do you mean?" thundered the Maulvi.

Shabnam was riding a high wave now. "What I am saying is Aslam cannot even get it up, so what am I to do?"

Aslam hitched his lungi and crossed his legs as if to hide the offending culprit. His ears burnt as he heard the sniggers and the barely concealed laughs. Allah! What had he got himself into? Did the bitch know what she was saying? Aslam felt the odds slowly piling up against him.

The Panchayat Mukhiya, still hopeful and thinking of the biryani said, "Shabnam Begum, your husband wants to divorce you because of your…er…wayward behaviour. Is this acceptable to you?"

"Rather late in the day to ask for my acceptance, Mukhiyaji. Can anyone prove I am an adulteress?" asked Shabnam.

"Aslam says so," said the Mukhiya with a finality that brooked no argument."

Shabnam laughed—"Aslam says and that is the final proof. Well if he says I am an adulteress then he must be right."

The Panchayat heaved a sigh of relief. Finally they were in control of the situation.

"Wait," thundered Shabnam. "Don't you want to know with whom I committed the terrible sin of adultery?"

The uneasy Mukhiya wanted to wind up the proceedings quickly but had to give in to the demands of the crowd that was fuelled by the vicarious pleasure of voyeurism.

Shabnam waited for silence. Turning to the Panchayat, she said with a deadpan face, "Mukhiyaji, have you forgotten that moonlit night in the sugarcane field? You may have forgotten how you squeezed me, but I haven't."

The Mukhiya blinked in shocked silence. He gulped, trying to speak, but Shabnam drove the arrow further in. "Maulviji, why don't you look at me now? When I came to sew for your wife, you could not take your eyes off me. And that mole on your chest. How you giggled when I touched it. My, and the weight of your belly, oof!"

The crowd was lapping it up with unholy glee at seeing the guardians of morality in the dock.

Shabnam sensed the mood of the crowd. "Mohammad Bhaijan, how can I call you 'Bhai' after that night? I will call you just 'Jan'."

"Stop, woman," shrieked the Maulvi. "You cannot prove all the slanderous things you say."

Shabnam said with an air of finality, "I say that you did it. You cannot prove otherwise."

Shabnam laughed at the discomfiture of the Panchayat. It was as if she had let loose a mischievous monkey in the crowd. Each one was trying to get away from the monkey.

"Maulviji, only my thighs and God know the truth." Shabnam picked up the money and jewels and walked away swaying her hips.

She did not even wait for the final pronouncement of *'talaq'* as she made her way out of the village. The village was agog with questions, unspoken and unanswered doubts. Had Shabnam spoken the truth? Was she just using bits of confidences and gossip shared at the village well? Was Aslam really impotent?

The Mukhiya was right. Nothing was the same again in Saidpur village.

Iced!

Sheena

Sheena put down the anthology of short stories and sat back as she mused on the story she read. A wife kills her unfaithful husband with the frozen beef piece and when the investigating officers are in the home looking for clues, she feeds them a steak cooked from the murder weapon. How gruesome! Could any wife actually bring herself to kill the man with whom she has shared life's intimate moments? How can the provocation be so great that you stoop to take away the life of one you love? But perhaps circumstances conspire in such a way that no other option is open. What circumstances, thought Sheena. If the man was a tyrant, perhaps some justification is there. But to kill him for being unfaithful, now that defied her imagination. Would I kill Rahul...Sheena stopped short. What am I thinking? How can I stoop to even think of such a thing?

The story had left her feeling low as Sheena opened the refrigerator dispiritedly. It was not working to full capacity as usual. They really needed a new frost free one. She sighed as she recalled the number of times that she had cajoled and nagged Rahul. Strange! Rahul once had been so house proud; once so palpably delighted to buy things for their little home; but now over the last two months he would be so preoccupied that he wouldn't notice anything in the house! Maybe he's missing a child, Sheena thought to herself, as she plonked on a chair. Seven years of marriage, but no child. Seven years of happiness tinged with apprehension and disappointment. I feel so inadequate, mused Sheena. I've somehow betrayed the one man that I love most. Somehow, somewhere I'm a half woman to a full man.

She dragged herself to the doctor next day for another appointment, for another hollow assurance; another half alive hope.

†

Sheena walked back home with a spring in her step, a glow on her face. Humming to herself, she drew back the curtains from the big bay windows, to let in the light. She was five weeks pregnant. Five weeks a tiny life had been growing within her and she was oblivious of the miracle. A bolt from the blue to jolt Rahul from his preoccupation.

She walked around the house setting everything right—flowers for the freshened and dusted rooms. She remembered to call for ice cubes from the home delivery store. Rahul liked a really chilled drink. Sheena's eyes were seeing dreams in fast forward motion. She waited impatiently to break the million-dollar news to Rahul. A police officer never came home in time.

When she saw his closed face, her heart sank a little. She wanted a perfect response to her momentous news. But her exhilaration was not dimmed for long. As she was going to the kitchen to get him a drink, Rahul stopped her, "Sheena, I've been wanting to tell you something. It's been playing on my mind for a long time. I don't know how to start." Sheena giggled to his surprise, "I too have something to tell you."

"Okay Sheena, you tell me your news."

"No, no Rahul, you tell me first." Sheena wanted her news to be an absolute climax, a torrent of happiness engulfing everything else. She could hardly sit still with the excitement building inside her.

Rahul blurted out, "Sheena I know this is going to hurt you, but it will be more hurtful to keep you in the dark. I am not happy in our relationship. No no, you're not at fault. You've been a great wife. But I met someone in Delhi a couple of months back, when I went for a seminar. Another police officer. I know this is sudden. But I can't seem to get her out of my mind. It's been like this for her too. I can't carry on any more. I want my freedom. I want to...."

Rahul looked shamefacedly at Sheena. She could hear a child crying in the distance. Something was hollow within her. She panicked. Where was her baby? Had the baby gone too? No, Rahul was the one who wanted to go, leaving this little life with her. Sheena looked wildly around her. Should she tell him her news? Would he stay back? But, why? I don't want a half-hearted father for my baby! Swift thoughts chased around in Sheena's mind. He had spoilt everything for me. How dare Rahul ruin the best thing in my life? Why did he have to do this today? What difference was the time and day going to make? Everything was finished.

Rahul looked at Sheena as she walked into the kitchen. He had an uncanny feeling. Why didn't she react? Had she registered the fact that everything was over between them?

Sheena opened the icebox. The ice cubes had hardened into a solid mass. She put it on the kitchen table to crush. Something snapped inside her. She deliberately put the ice mass into a double gauze bag and walked back into the drawing room. Rahul was sitting there exactly as she had left him, his back towards her. Sheena swung her arm back with all the force of betrayal and the venom of disappointment? Thud! The ice hit Rahul on his skull and he slumped forward. Sheena felt his pulse. He had gone off like a candle.

†

Sheena went back to the kitchen, washed the gauze bag free of blood stains, washed the ice carefully, put it back in the ice box and walked to her neighbour's house.

"Rekha, I need some ice cubes. The ice that I got from the store has solidified and it is such a pain to crush them. Rahul wants a chilled drink now."

Rekha's two year old daughter ran towards her. Sheena hugged her fiercely with the ecstasy of motherhood and the agony of frustrated wifehood welling up inside her. Sheena chatted for about 20 minutes since Rahul was taking a shower.

Sheena came back home. It was a shock to see Rahul sitting there stone dead. She screamed. Neighbours rushed in. Police came in swiftly for investigation. Two of the officers were Rahul's colleagues. They handled Sheena with kid gloves, even more when they knew her condition. Sheena sobbed hysterically. There was no pretence. Tragedy had struck her. Her child would never know its father. Ajay Malhotra and

Nagraj combed the house with a fine comb, but in vain. It was a clueless murder.

"Ajay, is Sheena's alibi fool proof?" Nagraj asked.

"Of course, I checked with the neighbours," replied Ajay Malhotra. "She was there between 6.30 pm and 7 pm. She was normal, nothing unusual. That was approximately the time of the murder. Besides what was the motive? They were looking forward to the baby. After seven years, it must have seemed like a miracle."

"Then who could have done it?" Nagraj wondered aloud. "Rahul seemed to have opened the door himself. When Sheena went out, the door locked automatically and she opened it again with her keys. So Rahul knew the murderer, since the door has not been forced open. He was murdered and the murderer went out closing the door behind."

Ajay looked around again. Where or rather what was the murder weapon? Something hard, dull but forceful. Something that could deliver a fatal blow. "Ajay, do you think this is a revenge murder?"

Ajay looked up swiftly. "Revenge? Could be that gangster who was released last week? Rahul had investigated the case and gathered the evidence that got him convicted."

†

The body was taken for post mortem.

Sheena seemed to have calmed down. She looked up dully. "Thanks Ajay for everything. You will take care of all the formalities won't you?"

"Of course Sheena, don't worry. I'll drop you to your sister's place. We should have informed her immediately."

Sheena went into the kitchen. Nagraj was there looking for a glass of water. "The refrigerator has not been working properly for some time." Sheena said apologetically. "I'll make you a soft drink".

With absolutely steady hands, she broke the ice from the icebox into pieces and made soft drinks for Ajay and Nagraj.

"What was the murder weapon?" wondered Ajay as he swirled the ice in the drink. Somehow he felt that the clue to this murder lay in identifying the weapon.

Sheena looked at the ice melting in the glasses. She had a hysterical urge to giggle. That was the end of Rahul. Now she knew what the circumstances could be to push a woman to murder. Should she have told him first, she mused.

"No. I am five weeks pregnant. While he was creating this miracle, his mind was on another woman." Sheena exulted. Nothing would mar her child's future. She was not a murderess. She was a mother.

In the kitchen Nagraj was searching the dust bin when he found the gauze bag.

Lighting the Darkness

Zayeda

"You good for nothing, where are you going when the evening lights are on?" Zayeda heard her mother-in-law's querulous voice from the room. Dipping the wick in the oil, she said, "I am going to place a lamp at the Shiva temple. Pandit Chacha asked me to, before he left the village." Zayeda's mother-in-law was speechless for a moment in the face of her daughter-in law's-temerity. "Light a lamp at the Shiva temple! Are you mad, woman? The militants threatened the Pandit with death if he did not leave the village; and now you are going to invite death by putting a lamp in the temple!"

"Ammi, I am only putting a lamp, so that the temple is not in darkness. What is the harm?"

"Harm. You'll do the whole family harm if you are stubborn. Will the militants forgive us?"

"How will the militants know that I have put the lamp?" asked Zayeda.

"Of course they will know. All through Kashmir, even the walls are their spies."

Zayeda went about her preparations, unconcerned at the storm that was breaking over her head. Her father-in-law too, joined in the tirade, to prevent her from going and putting a lamp in the Hindu temple. He had nothing against the temple or the deity. But fear for life, fear of retribution at the hands of the fanatic militants incited him to spout quasi philosophical arguments.

"For us there is none other than Allah. Now you will become a kafir, putting a lamp at the Shiva temple."

Zayeda turned on her in-laws with contempt.

"Kafir! Would you call Pandit Chacha a non-believer? Is he a kafir, just because he calls God Shiva and not Allah? Pandit Chacha prays all day and you call him a non-believer! You only told me that in 1971 the whole village prayed at the Shiva temple so that Pakistan would not bombard us. And millions of times you told your grandson that those prayers kept the village safe. Are all the villagers kafirs then?" Zayeda's in-laws were helpless in the face of their daughter-in-law's arguments. They resorted to authority. But in vain! Zayeda was hell bent on putting a lamp at the Shiva temple.

Their neighbour Shiv Prasad Bhat was the keeper of the small Shiva temple situated on a tiny hill near the village. In the face of death threats from the militants he, like many other Hindu Pandits was forced to flee, leaving the small Kashmiri village for Muslims alone. Before leaving with tears in his eyes, he had looked at Zayeda, "Beti, can you place a lamp every evening at the temple? I will feel happy knowing that my Shiva is cared for even though I am far away."

Zayeda held his hands. "Of course," she said. "This is a small thing that you are asking me."

"It is not small Beti. I don't know whether I am right in putting such a big responsibility on your young shoulders. But I have no choice. Shiva will protect you." Zayeda could never forget the look of despair on Pandit Chacha's face as he turned towards the temple for the last time.

†

Zayeda climbed the hill to the small temple. A Shiva lingam graced the small sanctum sanctorum. She cleaned the temple and lit the lamp. Suddenly the temple came to life with shadows dancing on the walls. After lighting the lamp, Zayeda was a bit confused on what to do next. She covered her head and recited verses from the Koran. Her chanting mingled with the wind among the firs as it echoed the holy verses. Zayeda felt a surge of peace within her as she sat in the twilight. From that day onwards, Zayeda climbed the hill every evening to put a lamp at the temple. She had to adjust her daily chores to make time for the added responsibility. Her in-laws maintained a disapproving silence. Her husband caught in the web of frustrated helplessness in the face of cruel militancy, saw this as a small gesture of defiance to the militants. He himself did not have the courage to actively support or stop Zayeda. But he grudgingly admitted her courage. His only warning to her was, "If you see suspicious characters around the temple, don't go there."

The villagers caught up in the violent times were clutching at any straw to keep their daily lives secure. They did not openly approve of Zayeda's gesture, but tacitly admitted to themselves that perhaps the small lamp would ward off the evil that was hanging over their heads.

Zayeda was getting used to the indifference and also to her mother-in-law's taunts when dinner was delayed.

"When does she have the time to cook? She is busy in her Punditain's role." The village *mukhiya* Basheer Lone came and remarked—

"Zayeda Begum, you are lighting the lamp in the temple at your own risk. If the militants from across the border come, don't expect the villagers to protect you."

But sadly the effect of his stern warning was diluted when Zayeda saw him surreptitiously bow his head in the direction of the temple.

For Zayeda the evening chore became the fulcrum of her life. In the beginning she climbed the hillock with a beating heart, keeping a lookout for the militants. But she also knew that militants rarely visited the temple. After lighting the lamp, she sat under the trees and recited her prayers. There amidst the trees, under the evening sky, with the small lamp lighting up the darkness, Zayeda felt nearer to Allah. Sitting there with the village in view, she could feel that all was well with the world and Allah would take care of everyone. No ideological conflict troubled her. Somehow, deep down in her heart she felt, that by lighting the lamp to Shiva, she was worshipping Allah.

A couple of times when she had heard suspicious noises from the forest, she had shut herself in the temple till the danger had passed. Once in the afternoon she saw a contingent of army soldiers going up to the temple. That evening she saw that some flowers and leaves had been placed at the Shiva lingam. From that day onwards Zayeda too placed flowers and leaves at the lingam.

†

One evening, about four months after Pandit Chacha had left the village, Zayeda had just placed the lamp inside the temple when she smelt danger. She turned and saw three figures in the half light. Her heart skipped several beats. Allah, is this my end? In the twilight she recognised Manzoor, the nephew of the school teacher. When he had been missing for a few months, it was said that he had gone across the border to be trained in militancy. With him were two figures, bearded, fearful and armed to the teeth.

Manzoor shouted, "Woman, are you mad or a kafir? Does a good Muslim light a lamp in the kafir's temple?"

Zayeda's legs were shaking. "Manzoor, are you a good Muslim, killing innocent people and destroying your land?"

The other two militants came threateningly close.

"How dare this woman talk to us like this? Just kill her and dump her body in the forest."

"Let's use her body first", leered the other frightful figure.

Zayeda's heart was in her mouth. Is this my end, dishonour at the hands of these devils. Allah, protect me. Her voice didn't shake a bit as she shouted derisively, "Rape and kill. That is the sign of a good Muslim, is it not? Remember this Shiva here is a powerful god of the Hindus. Touch me and you'll be blind before you're finished with me."

The last threat was a brainwave. Zayeda had no clue why she said it. But the three militants stopped for some time, whispering amongst themselves. One of them overcome by lust was scoffing at the others. Manzoor fearful of blindness or at least partial blindness if he supported the foreign militants was urgently arguing with them. He was reciting the miraculous incident when Shiva kept the village safe from Pakistan's bombs while many villages in the valley of Kashmir had been hit.

Zayeda drove home the advantage. "If you don't believe me, ask Manzoor. Six months back, a militant spent a night hiding in the temple. In the morning his dead body was found without a single bullet mark."

Manzoor wanted to get out of this sticky situation. He had no intention of earning the ire of the village, on finding that he was a party to Zayeda's murder. "Allah knows what my family might suffer at the hands of the villagers. Why can't these wretched foreign militants just stick to *jehad*?"

The two militants were still undecided. Their lust and their male ego could not take defiance from a woman. But to become blind and that too on enemy territory!

One of them told the other, "Why don't you go ahead? We will know whether her threat is true."

"Wah! I should be struck blind while you get away," shouted the other. Now fuelled by her own courage, Zayeda threw a challenge and cried out, "Come you devils! This is the last evening light you'll see, I promise you."

The militants decided to sacrifice their lust to their fear. But their egos had to be assuaged. "Let's just kill her."

"Kill me and when you go home, you'll find the woman nearest to your heart, dead." The militants stopped short.

"My mother dead!"

"My wife dead or perhaps my daughter."

Zayeda screamed, "Allah protects me. Shiva here is so powerful that he will reach up to your villages and destroy your homes. Shiva protects me too." The men decided to leave. Before going, to retain some vestige of their image as militants, they shot Zayeda in the legs. But she was alive.

†

Zayeda still limps up to the hill. She needs help. Her friends from the village help her up to the temple, where Zayeda had been saved. After Zayeda lights the lamp, the women gather there and recite the Koran. Sitting there Zayeda often wonders—"Did Allah protect me that day? Did Shiva come to my rescue? Or did mere superstition save the day?"

Change of Masters

Shanti

"This milk is too hot," the querulous voice pierced Shanti's ears. Yesterday the milk was too cold. Shanti wearily rose to her feet to cool the milk and stopped suddenly. She looked around and saw the neatly made vacant bed. He was no more. It was two months since Shanti's husband had died. But a lifetime's habits die hard. Married for 51 years Shanti had served and served her husband. That was the sum total of their relationship. He was the master and demanded service. She served to her utmost capacity. Of course he loved her for the unquestioning loyalty. And possibly for the unquestioning physical service. Where in the humdrum existence of caring for husband, children and in-laws was there an opportunity to question? She only heard the answers to questions she never dared or cared to voice.

For Shanti it was quite impossible to comprehend that she had finally retired from a half century of service, unpaid, unrecognised, unappreciated. Fifty one years of being taken for granted by husband and children. She was always there to cook and care, to wash and wish away ills; to run the house even when everyone ran out every morning; to hold fort when everything seemed to crumble in a crisis. Now finally she was alone and free. She regretted her husband's death, but she was thankful too. She often caught herself up guiltily when she felt relieved that she did not have to get up at night to change the hot water bottle. She was slowly discovering the excitement of deciding her own menu, the pleasure of watching an uninterrupted programme on the TV without being asked to fetch and carry a million times.

"Amma you cannot stay in this huge house all alone. It is not safe," said Shanti's son irritably, thinking of the huge money blocked in the house. "Ammaji, we will make you very comfortable with us," said her younger daughter-in-law, thinking how easy life would be if she did not have to leave the children in the crèche every day. "Perhaps Amma wants to stay here since it has Papaji's memories," interrupted Shanti's daughter, unwilling to let go of a refuge that she could come to when life got too much for her. Shanti caught on, "I don't want to leave this house. I feel your Papaji is still here. No I don't want anyone to live with me." Her sons droned on about the insecurity of old people living alone, the rising expenses and the foolishness of running two establishments.

Shanti was getting exasperated. Why did they persist in explaining extensively to her as if she was a child? She who had brought them up to adulthood was now being treated like a child. She who ran a huge home on limited income was now being taught the nuances of cost efficient living. It was as if with her husband her intelligence was also taken away. True, all major decisions had been taken for her. But she had the intelligence to make her own decisions, now that she had the opportunity, didn't she? She looked at her two sons and saw how dangerously close they were to their father. "Petty tyrants" she thought.

She looked at her daughters-in-law and felt their minds click in conniving strategies. Shanti was sure. She did not want to exchange one tyrant for another; to leave her space and be an intruder in her daughter-in-law's space. She felt that somehow, she could not take a minute more of adjustment.

"Your Papaji left this house and money to me. As long as I am alive and well, I will live in this house. Shankar and his wife are living in the servant quarters. That is enough security for me. I will not come to live with anyone just now." Her children looked at her as if she had taken leave of her senses.

†

Alone that night, Shanti thought of her life and what she wanted to do with the few years left to her. She felt like a convict on parole who wants to make most of his freedom and savour every moment of his liberty. With retirement from her 24x7 job, Shanti could only savour the pleasant sense of anticipation. She bought a CD player and watched Hindi and English movies continuously for a month. It was a relief not to be bound by the relentless pressure of planning and cooking three meals. She ate when she felt like and for the first time planned menus according to her fancy. She was 70, but in her new found freedom she felt 50. Her sons were uneasy. Her daughters-in-law sniggered at her. Relatives advised her gently. Shanti did not care. She had spent a lifetime imprisoned by others' opinions. Now she cared only for her own opinion.

Then came the final straw, as far as her sons were concerned. Their mother applied and got her passport. A passport! Without even asking her sons! Where did she want to go at this age? And why? What about the expense?

"I am not asking you to fund me," said Shanti belligerently.

"You'll spend all the money and come back empty handed to us," said her sons.

"I am not such a fool. If I could teach you to be careful with your money, I should know how to spend carefully." Shanti wanted them to be gone, so that she could pore over the travel brochures. She had found a conducted tour for the 60 plus, to take them to South East Asia. She had signed up for the tour along with her brother. He was a widower and like her, free of any encumbrances. Three weeks of sightseeing, shopping, sampling exotic fare, reading and just doing nothing. Shanti came back, satiated, happy and still excited. Her brother had been a great help with the passports, itineraries, and the luggage. He came back with her and stayed on since there was no immediate need for him to go back to his home and family. Besides he liked the big house and the calm ordered life.

†

Shanti liked having a man in the house. She had unconsciously missed the masculine towels hanging on the clothes rail. She enjoyed planning a menu keeping another taste in mind. She welcomed once more the smell of the cigars intermingling with the fragrance on incense. She enjoyed hearing the early morning whistling. Now and then she changed the bed covers on her husband's bed, and shed a few tears. She thought of him, but did not miss him tragically.

"Shanti, this drink is too chilled. Take out a few ice cubes," her brother's brusque voice reached her in the kitchen. Why can't he take out the ice cubes and leave it on the tray, she thought to herself. Shanti spooned out the cubes. Next morning she packed her brother's clothes and called for a taxi.

"Bhai, you must not leave your home and children for too long. I have told them that you are going today."

As the taxi drove away, Shanti opened her travel brochures. This time she would travel alone. And then…"I am free…free to decide for myself".

Dear Enemy

Dildar

"You are late, Dildar. We have nearly finished our washing." Asmat and her friends were rinsing the last of their washing as Dildar walked to the river edge with her pile of dirty clothes.

"Today I got really late because, I was cleaning out the cow shed."

"When you have sold off the cow, then why do you have to clean the cowshed?"

"We might buy another cow, Inshallah!!"

The other women kept silent, allowing Dildar the comfort of her dreams. Everybody in the village of Bhedi Kalan knew that Dildar's husband Ali had been out of a job for four months while he recovered from the dreaded tuberculosis. It was only recently that he managed to get a job as a daily wage farm hand. It was a hand to mouth existence and the women had seen the bloom in Dildar's cheeks fade. Dildar carefully stepped over the rocks and started soaping the clothes on a big slab. The current in the Sutlej was dangerous, and Dildar was careful to remain near the bank.

Life had been tough for Dildar. The small piece of land had been mortgaged, and the cow sold off to meet the expense of medicines. The big brass vessel and the jug with the glasses had been sold off to buy nutrition for Ali. Dildar thought of selling off her wooden cot that her parents had given her for the marriage.

It would fetch a good price, she thought and they could buy milk and meat for some more time. Doctor Sahib had said that if he did not eat well, the medicines would eat him. Hai Allah, when would they be free of these worries? Dildar's thoughts raced as her hands mechanically scrubbed, rinsed and squeezed the clothes. It was past noon and not a soul was seen on the riverbank. An air of somnolence hung over the village, as people shut their doors against the hot sun. In the distant Dildar could see mothers shepherding the reluctant children indoors. A little further away she could hear the school children reciting sleepily.

†

"Help," Dildar heard a faint voice. She stopped washing and looked around her. "Help me. I am drowning." The cry was unmistakable. Dildar looked at the river and saw a man struggling in the current. Hai Allah, he will surely drown, she thought to herself. The current that side was treacherous. Dildar ran on the bank and saw that the man was clinging to a large rock. But the current was pulling at him, trying to prise him away from the rock into its fatal arms. Dildar looked towards the village. She could see nobody. The men were away in the fields. She realised that she had no time to run for help. For a moment Dildar was numb. The man looked at the end of his tether as he battled with the current, clinging desperately to the rock. Dildar raced on the bank to the point nearest to the drowning man. But she was too far off to help him. Further down, the river curved sharply. If he could come near the bank, she could haul him up.

"Pull away from the rock," she shouted trying to make herself heard above the roar of the river. "Further the river curves, try to come nearer to the bank" Shouting and gesticulating desperately, Dildar made herself understood. She ran to the curve of the river, and looked around for a rope or branch of a tree. Weeping willows hung on the bank, but Dildar did not have a knife to cut down the branches. There wasn't even enough time to try with her bare hands. Dildar knew that any second the man would come round the curve.

Allah help me to help this poor man. There are only a few seconds to pull him up before the current drags him further. Give me strength Allah, Dildar prayed in desperation.

She could see the man's arms and legs flailing as he rounded the corner, the raging current trying hard to pull him away. Around the curve, he was nearest to the bank. Dildar could almost see the desperation in his eyes, as she threw her cotton dupatta towards him. By a stroke of luck, the drowning man grabbed the dupatta, in the first attempt. Dildar pulled hard with all her might, trying slowly to pull him to the bank. It took every ounce of her strength, to battle against the raging current as she pulled the full-grown man. Pulling him by inches she brought him almost near the bank. It was a herculean task to hang on to the dupatta, while the river was hell bent on snatching it from her. She tied her end of the dupatta to the weeping willow and then resumed pulling. Sweat rivulets crept down her face as her sore hands pulled hard. The man clung to the dupatta. Slowly he was pulling his way to the bank. At one point Dildar's heart almost stopped as an especially strong current hit the man pulling his legs away from the bank. Dildar stopped and tried hard to look for his head that had gone underwater. After what seemed like several minutes, she saw him surface, coughing and spluttering, but hanging on to the dupatta for life.

"*Shabaash,* just a few feet more. I will pull you through," Dildar encouraged the man who seemed to be almost fainting. Dildar pulled him up to the bank and helped him onto the dry ground. He collapsed in a heap and lay motionless. Dildar panting, was worn out with the effort. She looked closely to see that he was breathing. Relieved she sat next to him waiting for him to come around.

Bedraggled though he was, Dildar could make out that he belonged to a well-off family. Two gold rings sat tightly on his ring fingers. He was fair and his hair was tightly cropped. Where was he from? How did he fall into the river? Where was his family? They must be looking for him. Dildar's thoughts raced as she got her breath back. Slowly the man opened his eyes groggily and tried to sit up. He looked at Dildar and smiled; a smile that started slowly from the lips and then lit up his entire face.

"Thank you. But for you I would be dead and food for the fishes by now."

"Allah saved you," Dildar said simply.

The smile vanished from the man's face and he looked warily at her.

"Where am I? What is the name of the village there?"

"That is the village of Bhedia Kalan, my village,"

The man groaned, as if in tremendous pain and put his head in his hands while his shoulders shook with dry sobs.

"God did you save me from the river to push me into hell?"

"Hell, what do you mean? My village is comfortable. We even have a health centre."

"Can I call you Behenji? Well then, let me get back into the river. A watery death is acceptable to me."

Dildar looked puzzled. The man looked at her for some time.

"I am an officer of the Indian army. You have saved my life. So I hope you will not betray me to your Pakistan army. You can of course make a hue and cry. The Pakistan Rangers will take me away, torture me and then kill me, since I am an enemy officer. But then your effort in saving me would be futile."

†

Dildar sat down. Hai Allah, I have saved an Indian man! Only last year there had been a war between Pakistan and India. The Indian army had shelled their village on the Pakistan border. Afzal Khan along with three of his cousins had been killed in their fields. The fire had destroyed the crops on the other side of the village too. Jabeena's cattle shed had caught fire and six houses on the side of the well had been destroyed. For two weeks, people had left their villages to take shelter with their relatives or in the wooded areas. When they came back, they found that miscreants had looted many of the houses. It was the worst nightmare that the village faced collectively, for being close to the border between Pakistan and India. In the village of Bhedia Kalan, calling a man Indian was almost an abuse. Dildar looked at the man who was looking at her, hope and fear mingled in his eyes. If I leave him here, he will definitely be handed over to the Pakistani Rangers, she thought. But where could she take him?

If she took him home, what would her husband say? Besides how would she hide him and for how long? How would she be able to send him back? She had no money. Why should she save him? But she had already saved him from the river. Could she send him to a sure death? If she hid him, and the Rangers found out, then they would kill her and Ali. Besides he was an enemy!

Dildar battled with her thoughts. She sat near the undergrowth to talk to the stranger.

"You are in great danger here. This is a border village and the Pakistani Rangers are constant visitors. If anyone sees you, then it is sure death. Everyone in this village considers Indians as enemies."

The man was silent for a moment. "Behenji, I know the danger that I am in and I don't want to put you in any kind of trouble. The border is close by. If I can stay here till night, then I can slip past the sentries into the Indian side"

"But how will you find your way at night?"

"I will have to take a risk."

"You stay here. Let me think up a plan. But don't come out of your hiding, no matter what happens. Come out only when I call. What is your name?"

"Arjun Singh. And your name?"

"Dildar. Dildar Begum. Remember don't come out, no matter what happens."

Dildar gathered her washing up and raced home. Her thoughts raced with her. What madness was this Dildar? Why should you save an enemy? He is just an unfortunate man. But he belongs to the army that put your village through so much of misery. He must have been following his orders. She was sure their soldiers would also be bombing Indian villages. After going through so much trouble to save him from the river, she couldn't send him to his death.

But suppose somebody got to know, she would be branded as a traitor. Then Allah alone could save her. Despite the dilemma, Dildar somehow felt responsible for Arjun's safety.

Sitting and brooding endlessly was not in Dildar's character. As soon as she hung up the washing, she sat down to make a few rotis. She packed the potato curry that she had made for herself, with the rotis. She quickly emptied the water pot and placed it on her head to bring water from the river. She needed a plausible excuse for going to the river again. She quickly rummaged through Ali's clothes. She took out a *pathan* suit that had been made at the last Eid. Carrying the small packet of food and the clothes, she quickly made her way to the river. She went to the thick undergrowth and sat at the river bank. She looked all around. Not a soul was on the bank. She called softly, "Saheb". There was no response to her second and third call. Dildar's heart missed a beat. Had he been discovered? Was he a prisoner? She went closer to the clump of grass. "Arjun Saheb, come out it is I, Dildar." There was a slight movement and she could see a pair of eyes peering cautiously at her.

"I have brought you some food" Arjun took the rotis and ate hungrily.

"We have to think of a way to keep you safe."

"At night I will make my way out. Somehow I have to find the way to the border."

"That is easier said than done. Listen to me. You wait here till it is dark. Then I will come with my husband to take you home. It is safer to hide there than in the open like this."

"Behenji, why will your husband allow me in his house? Besides how will I get to the border?"

"I can talk to him. He will be able to think of a solution." Dildar sounded more confident than she felt.

"Now you change into these clothes, so that you don't stand out if anyone chances to see you." Dildar gathered the discarded Indian army uniform and bundled it into her bag. She filled her water pot and warned Arjun again, even as she said a quick prayer for his safety.

†

That evening Dildar prepared Ali's favourite dish, the *baingan bharta*. She sat next to him, fanning him while he ate his fill. Once she heard his satisfied burp, she narrated the highlight of the day. Ali was dumbstruck.

"Dillu are you insane? Do you even realise what you have done? Your stupidity will ruin us."

"I could not leave him to drown could I?"

"But you could have called for help."

"There was no time. Besides if the villagers caught him, you know what his fate would be. The *lambardar* would hand him over to the Rangers and claim reward for himself."

"But Dillu, he is an enemy."

"But he is a human being. He has done us no harm!"

"But his country has. Worse still he is a *fauji*."

"Yes, the Indian army has shelled our village. Our soldiers must have also done harm to the Indian villages."

"But Dillu, what are we to do with him?"

"We will think of something once he is safe in the house."

"I don't want an Indian *fauji in* my house." Ali stated firmly. He saw Dildar's set face and his heart sank. "How will we hide him and till when?"

"That you leave to me. But I will not allow him to be handed over for certain death." Ali kept quiet, cowed down by Dildar's assertive character. He knew that Dildar was a doer, and once she had made up her mind to do something, it was infinitely less tiring to fall in with her plans. Ali could not even dare to think of the horrifying consequences of her actions. Both husband and wife waited till there was silence in the village, and then stealthily walked up to the river bank.

"Arjun Saheb, come out," whispered Dildar softly, while Ali kept watch. Capt. Arjun Singh crawled out of the clump of grass and stretched himself painfully. Ali quickly motioned to him to walk towards the village.

Dildar whispered urgently, "If anyone sees us, you are my cousin from my village and you are dumb from birth."

Ali marvelled at Dildar's ingenuity. Quietly the trio made their way home. The village dogs barked, but no one stirred. In the flickering lamp, Ali looked at the tall good looking Indian officer and flinched when he saw his best pathan suit. He looked at Dildar who smiled warily. Arjun looked at the humble hut and felt humbled by the courage of the couple before him. All three stood awkwardly trying to assess the situation. Dildar broke the silence first.

"Saheb, you must be hungry." Arjun interrupted her. "Since I am your cousin, stop calling me Saheb and call me Bhai, and yes I am very hungry."

†

Dildar busied herself laying out the simple meal of rotis and *baingan bharta.* She watched him as he ate. Strangely she did not fear what the future would bring. She had no clue how they were going to help him to cross the border to his own country. She was not even sure how she would hide him from prying eyes. But she felt a sense of elation and an optimism that somehow things would get sorted out. Ali sat in a corner, watching the unwelcome guest. His mind was scampering in all directions, trying to work out ways by which the guest could be sent away as fast as possible.

After dinner, Arjun said, "I do realise Ali that I am unwelcome here and I am subjecting both of you to grave danger. But I need a roof for a few hours till I figure out my directions. Can you help me?"

Dildar waited with bated breath for Ali's answer.

"Sahebji, Allah has brought you here and as a guest in my house. We will take care of you. As far as directions go, the border is not far from here. If we walk up the river, we will reach the point where it enters Pakistan. But it is impossible to cross the border. The Pakistani Rangers keep a vigil all the time. Besides when the Indian soldiers spot anyone crossing the border, they shoot, even before you identify yourself."

Arjun was silent as he assimilated the sticky situation he was in.

"Something can be worked out, I think," Ali said slowly.

"There is this man who smuggles stuff from India and sells it in the cities. He probably knows points where the border is easy to cross."

"But why will he risk his life?"

"He risks his life every time he crosses the border. I think he will do it for money."

"But I lost my purse in the river. Only my identity card is safe, as it was pinned to my uniform."

Dildar looked anxious. They would never be able to get enough money to pay the smuggler.

"But I have this gold ring. Maybe you can sell it and raise money."

Arjun took off the smaller of his two rings and gave it to Ali. Ali took it slowly, wondering what he would explain to the jeweller. A fine ring in Ali's house was sure to cause suspicion. Dildar reading his thoughts said–

"Do you know where to catch hold of the smuggler? First let us see how much money he will ask for. Then you can sell this ring in the town nearby. If anyone asks, you can say we are selling it for medicines."

"The smuggler is usually seen at Karim Chacha's tea shop, unless he has gone across the border."

"Suppose he betrays you?" Dildar asked, worried.

"He won't want to get involved with the Rangers since he is a smuggler, and he will do anything for money."

Sleep eluded Dildar that night as she devised ways and means to keep Arjun hidden from her neighbours and friends.

†

Dildar woke up before daybreak, stealthily locked her door and made her way to the river. It was eerie as the waters glistened in the cold moonlight. Before the village stirred to life she had washed the clothes and brought the water from the river. By the time it was daylight, Dildar had woken up Ali and packed his lunch. After seeing him off, she quickly cleaned the tiny attic where wood was stored for her kitchen and helped Arjun up there after giving him a meagre breakfast of tea and roti. Sitting in her tiny kitchen space, Dildar could look up and see Arjun curled up. While cooking, she told Arjun about her husband's illness, their hopes to regain their land and buy a cow. Arjun in turn narrated how during the course of mock war exercise, he was supervising the building of a pontoon bridge across the Sutlej. He along with two soldiers had fallen into the river.

That day a simple village woman from Pakistan and an army officer from India bonded over their fortunes and misfortunes.

†

"Dildar, Dildar, where are you?" Dildar quickly motioned to Arjun to hide. She messed up her hair and tied a dupatta on her forehead. She then opened the door for Jabeena.

"What happened Dildar, I have not seen you since morning? Why have you locked the door? Why have you tied a dupatta on your head? Do you have a headache?"

"Oof, oh Jabeena, you are like a train running on and on with questions. Yes I have a bad headache and that is why I locked the door to keep out the noise. I was resting."

"Can I help you? I came to tell you that the Rangers were here this morning on a patrol."

Dildar's heart leapt into her mouth. She clenched her clammy hands. Rangers? Why were they here? She tried to make her voice sound as normal as possible, which was difficult since she felt she could not breathe properly.

"Oh the usual inspection and the routine questions on whether any stranger was seen in the border village. In such a small village can any stranger hide and escape detection?"

"Exactly. Jabeena I will talk to you once I am feeling better." Dildar shepherded Jabeena out and locked the door, heaving a sigh of relief.

†

It was the longest day of Dildar's life. She thought of all the calamities that could befall Ali and swung like a pendulum between hope and hopelessness. Somehow she got through the day, chatting to Arjun about his home and sisters. By mutual consent they did not talk about the enmity between the two countries. In any case it seemed out of place in the small hut where a soldier from one nation had taken refuge and a woman from another was orchestrating his escape. Ali returned well after dark. Dildar could hardly wait for him to come inside, before she started bombarding him with questions.

"Sahebji, I have good news for you," said Ali. "Vilayat Khan the smuggler is willing to take you across the border for 20,000 rupees. I was able to sell your ring for 25,000 rupees. I have given an advance to Vilayat Khan, the rest is to be given after you get into Indian territory. Here is the balance money. But you have to go tonight itself"

"Tonight? But where will Sahebji go?"

"After midnight we will have to walk upriver till we reach two big rocks directly opposite a white mosque with a single minaret. He will meet us there."

"Ali thank you. This is excellent news," responded Dildar excitedly. "But do you think this Vilayat Khan can be trusted? Suppose he turns Sahebji over to the Rangers or kills him for the money?"

"Dillu, you think I am an idiot! I told him that he would get the rest of the money only after Sahebji is convinced that he is in Indian territory. Once inside Indian territory, a smuggler like him will not dare do anything to attract attention to himself. Besides what will he gain by killing him?"

"Behenji, I will have to trust someone or the other," Arjun sounded convinced. "This is my only chance."

†

Dildar went to the riverside to fill water. She gave a start as she heard a jeep

"Bibi you should not come for water so late in the evening. It is not safe in a border village." The Pakistani Ranger officer along with three men was on his patrol.

"Salaam Sahebji. Today I got late since I had a headache. But I won't do this again. Where are you going Sahebji so late?" The normally reticent Dildar became quite garrulous in an attempt to find out the patrol's movements.

"Our duty is arduous, trying to keep you folks safe from those conniving Indians. We are on our way to the next village."

"Sahebji would you and your men like a drink of water? It is hot and you must be thirsty. Next village, down the river or up the river Sahebji?"

The unusually friendly village woman pleasantly surprised the Ranger.

"Yes I am thirsty. Now we will go to the village down the river."

Dildar hurried home to give the information. Arjun once again wondered at Dildar's great initiative.

Late that night, Arjun accompanied by Ali and Dildar stealthily made their way up the river, making sure to keep in the shadow of the trees. Arjun still wore Ali's pathan suit to avoid danger. He gave his identity card to Dildar for safe keeping till he reached the border. He was glad Dildar was accompanying them. It made them less suspicious. Moreover in that short time span, he had developed a great faith in her resourcefulness. At her insistence he had already practised his deaf and dumb act, to avoid detection if questioned. Dildar had already decided, if questioned, to say that she was on a pilgrimage to the single minaret mosque to pray for her husband's health. She wanted to be in the mosque for the first namaaz at daybreak. Really there was no end to her ingenuity, thought Ali to himself in wonder. All three walked silently. Dildar could hear her heart beat, as she recited her prayers. She almost died with fright, when they saw two men coming towards them. Ali motioned them into a small wooded area. The two drunkards staggered, singing merrily, oblivious of the nocturnal walkers. Ali waited for some more time and gestured them to move. They reached the two large rocks on the bank of the river, directly opposite to the mosque in the distance. Dildar could see the faint outline of the minaret in the moonlight. They waited in the shadows, not daring to breathe, while Ali skirted the trees looking cautiously for Vilayat Khan. He saw the burning tip of a cigarette. Stealthily Ali went forward and breathed easy as he saw Vilayat Khan.

"Ali as long as I live I will never forget what you have done for me. May Allah shower his grace on you," said Arjun, hugging him tight.

"Dildar Behenji, you are truly well named. You are large hearted and you are the special sister that Allah gave me. I will remember you in every prayer that I say."

With tears in her eyes, Dildar whispered brokenly, "May Allah keep you safe Bhaijan."

Arjun walked away as the darkness swallowed him and Vilayat Khan.

At daybreak, Dildar said her namaaz in the mosque and prayed fervently for the Indian soldier's safety. On reaching home, she went to her small kitchen to make tea and spied a small packet near her pots. Dildar found Arjun's other gold ring and 5000 rupees. She sobbed, her two-day old stress overtaking her. She sobbed for the bond forged within a few hours. A few days later, Ali brought the news that Vilayat Khan had seen Arjun safely into Indian territory. Dildar thought that the story was finished.

Eight months later, she was called to the post office to collect a money order from India. The postmaster read out the message that the money was in gratitude for the kindness shown to one Arjun Singh's parents by Dildar's family. Arjun had kept Dildar's secret safe.

Every month till she lived, the money orders kept coming to remind Dildar of her brother across the border.

The Tiger's Dinner

Parvati

Parvati had a premonition of danger since morning when she packed a meal for her husband. He was going to the town and would return the next day. Perhaps it was her post pregnancy condition that was making her feel depressed. Left alone in the tiny mud hut in the little village of the district of 24 Parganas in West Bengal, Parvati felt like weeping. It was not the first time that her husband left her alone to go to the city to earn a few rupees more by lifting loads at the dock. The little patch of land was just enough to feed them, and now with the child they needed so much more money. The little thatched hut contained Parvati's world. After almost three years of marriage and innumerable taunts on her 'barrenness' Parvati had given birth to a baby girl. Durga Ma had come to bless their small home.

Parvati sat down at the doorway to massage the baby with warm mustard oil. It was a bright sunny day and Parvati could see the water logged fields as far as the eye could see. Far away to the west she could see the hut of her nearest neighbour. Further the fields gave way to the marshy land of the Sunderbans forest. She could never look at the forest without feeling a chill in her spine. Her father had been killed by the tiger in the same forest when he went to collect honey. Even his body could not be traced. Parvati had grown up, hearing stories of feline cunningness. She knew how the Sunderbans tiger camouflaged perfectly well in the marshy terrain, only to reveal himself before the hapless victim. Her father had been sitting on the stern of the boat when the tiger had silently pulled him into the water. The boatman sitting a few feet away had not seen or heard anything. Yet, when Parvati had seen the body of the dead maneater being taken away by the forest department, she had felt a wave of sympathy for the magnificent creature. He killed to eat, and Parvati who had often felt the pangs of hunger, empathised with the Sunderban tiger.

Parvati hummed a song as she swaddled her baby and rocked her to sleep. The baby smiled sleepily at her and Parvati's heart contracted with joy. She was only a few days old, yet Parvati felt completely connected to her.

†

Parvati could not shake off her sense of uneasiness, as she went about her daily chores. She was alone with the baby for the first time. Suppose, she fell ill or choked over her milk!! The pragmatist in Parvati shooed away all fears. But her uneasiness persisted. Maybe I should call Lakshmi from the village to stay with me at night, thought Parvati. Then she remembered that Lakshmi's mother-in-law was ill. I wish I had my mother or mother-in-law with me. Both had died last year of malaria. Sitting in the afternoon sun, drying her hair, Parvati resumed stitching old cotton saris into a blanket for the coming cold months. Today the silence was terrifying her. She could hear the chirping of the birds and the swishing of the leaves, but she could not hear the assuring tones of human voices. Parvati had never felt lonely before. She had always liked the solitude of her home away from the closed confines of the village street, away from the jealous gossip and the curious questions. Parvati knew in her heart that had she been living in the village, the taunts on her barrenness would have made her life miserable. Should she take the baby, and go to Lakshmi's house for the night? Parvati's mind vascillated. What would she tell Lakshmi? That she was frightened of staying alone? Her baby's cries would keep the ailing old lady awake. No she would have to stay in the little hut. Durga Ma would protect her.

In the afternoon, Parvati cut some wood and collected dry twigs to light a fire. Before sunset itself she brought the dried clothes inside and fastened the small door of the thatched hut. As dusk approached, she lit a fire outside the door to keep away any animal predator. Parvati knew through experience, that animals, particularly tigers were petrified of the fire. Through a small opening on top of the door she threw twigs to keep the fire burning. With the approach of the night, Parvati's fears multiplied. Suppose some drunkard passing by walked into the house. The door was scant protection. What if a hungry tiger came near the hut? Parvati's heart shivered as she thought of her baby's fate in the mouth of a hungry tiger. Quite often the hungry tigers strayed out from the Sunderban forests into human habitation and slunk away with goats, cows and even humans. Last year, Babla, the tea vendor's nephew had been killed by the tiger as he went to the fields to relieve himself. Before that, the tiger had entered the goat pen in Alam's house. After every incident the forest officers, the 'jungle *babus*' came, held meetings with the *panchayat*, the block development officers and then went away. The village talked of the incident for a few days and then all was normal, even for the bereaved family.

Parvati's mother had often told her—"The tiger is more scared of us than we are of him. But he is even more scared of hunger. When his stomach is empty, he is foolhardy and will even face the guns."

Parvati knew well that hunger drove the tigers into the village. The tigers killed people and slunk away into the forest. But the man-eater was hardly ever caught, even though the forest conservators assured the village that the tiger would be trapped and taken to the zoo. That, as far as Parvati could remember, had never happened. But the villagers were always threatened with dire consequences if a tiger was killed by them. The government would protect the tigers, but the villagers had to fend for themselves when they went about collecting honey, fishing, gathering wood, plants and fruits from the forest. Perhaps it was the tigers who voted the government into power, thought Parvati wryly.

†

Parvati lit the small lamp in front of the coloured picture of the goddess in her resplendent fury.

"Ma protect my baby and me. Help me to get through this night safely." Parvati wondered why this prayer came out spontaneously. There was no danger lurking around the corner. Yet her heart felt uneasy. Parvati scraped the last morsel of rice and spinach from the bottom of the mud pot. She sat motionless for a moment. What was that sound? It seemed as if someone was breathing deeply. No her imagination was playing tricks on her again. She got up to look at the baby sleeping peacefully in the corner.

There again that sound of deep breathing. She looked all around, but saw nothing. She adjusted the wick of the hurricane lamp and looked at the burning fire in the doorway. She fed the fire with a few more twigs. Perhaps it was the crackling sound that she had heard.

Parvati spread the mat on the floor and as she looked up, her heart missed a beat. Through the small window on the wall she saw a pair of gleaming eyes. She had never ever seen such a malevolent pair of eyes. As her eyes adjusted to the darkness, she realised with horror that she was looking into the face of a tiger. He was standing on his hind legs to look through the window. It was a very small aperture, and he could not squeeze through. He was panting and breathing heavily. Saliva was dripping from his open mouth as he looked at his prey. Parvati felt her feet were made of lead. Her first instinct was to pick up the baby and run outside. Her numbed brain rejected it as she realised, it would be a matter of seconds before the tiger pounced on her. She looked fearfully at the door. She knew that as far as the fire was burning, the tiger would not attempt to crash open the door. How long would it be before the tiger overcome by hunger would use his strength to get into the house? Parvati knew that if the tiger jumped onto the roof, he could drop down through the meagre thatched roof into the small room. And then!!! Parvati's mind could not even grasp the consequences. Her mouth was dry with fear. Should she throw a bucket of water to stun him? And after that, what? Fuelled by anger, he would be even more ferocious. Why had he come to her house, when Lakshmi's house was closer to the forest? Parvati puzzled over it. In the throes of her fear, Parvati remembered old wives' tales of the tiger's taste for the flesh of new born babies, and how they could smell the fresh natal blood from far off. Ma Durga, did you give me a baby after so long for this ill fate? Parvati knew that she too would end up in the tiger's stomach.

Parvati looked at the window again. The tiger was no longer there. She looked at the door fearfully. Once again the tiger appeared at the window. Parvati looked at the face of death and made a resolve. She was not going to give up her baby to those terrible fangs. "I am going to fight. Ma Durga, give me the strength!"

She looked around for a suitable weapon. The sickle that she used for cutting grass lay in a corner. Parvati considered it in her mind and rejected it. To use the sickle on the tiger she would have to get close to him, and Parvati knew that she was no match for his sharp teeth and strong paws. Almost mechanically, Parvati put a big piece of wood into the fire and saw the flames leaping up. The fire could be their saviour. But how? Could she use a burning twig to frighten him off? But for how long. She could not get too close; else he would snatch at her. Parvati saw the tiger's saliva dripping through the window. He was silent except for his rasping breath. He too was planning his attack. Tiger's cunningness and Parvati's wits were pitched against each other.

Parvati spotted an iron rod in the corner of the house. She had brought it inside the house the previous evening, thinking that any wandering tramp could steal it. Parvati thanked Fate for a swift second. There was no time to lose. Parvati knew that the tiger's patience would run out and he would find a way to attack. At the moment it seemed he was feasting on the sight and smell of the prospective dinner, before actually tasting it. Could she use the iron rod to hit at the tiger? If she wounded him, it could be terrifying. A wounded tiger's anger knew no bounds. She had to frighten him off. But how? The tiger was watching every move of hers with his cold, cruel eyes. Now and then he tried to squeeze his head further through the tiny window. Parvati hoped the dried mud wall would stand firm. The rasping sound from his throat seemed deafening to her ears. But he did not roar, since intuitively he did not want to attract unwelcome attention. Perhaps he knew that Parvati and her baby were easy prey.

Parvati took the iron rod purposefully and through the slit in the door, held it over the fire. Slowly the rod heated up. Parvati wrapped a wet cloth over her hands to hold the rod. It seemed like eternity before she saw the rod glow red hot. She waited for it to heat further. It had to be just right. If too hot, then the rod would be soft and useless against her target. If too cold, it would not ward the predator. The rod glowed red, almost as malevolently as the tiger's eyes. Parvati could see the tigers fangs as he panted open mouthed. She thought the red hot rod would wound the tiger and in pain he would rush off to his familiar terrain, the forest. Parvati held the rod and purposefully crept up to the window. She stood up and with all the force of her motherhood, hit the man-eater with the molten red rod. It slipped into the tiger's open mouth and the burning hot rod stuck deep in his gullet. Parvati heard a terrible roar and saw the writhing tiger slip down. She could hear him crashing through the under growth, his guttural roar of pain echoing in the darkness. Parvati slipped more wood into the fire. In its glow she could see the shadowy figure of the tiger bounding blindly in pain. She held her baby tight and kept her eyes fixed to the door. Would he come back to extract revenge? What had she done? Had she killed him or wounded him for life? A maimed tiger was a bigger threat to the village, handicapped as he was from hunting the prey in the forest. Ma Durga forgive me, I had no other way.

†

The whole night through, Parvati kept an uneasy vigil, clinging to her baby and feeding the vital fire at the doorway. She opened the door late into the morning and saw unusual activity near the edge of the forest. Officials were driving up to the forest. The rumble of the jeeps struck Parvati cold. Shading her eyes, she saw her husband coming down the tracks between the fields. She waited for him with bated breath.

"Paro, a tiger has been killed, in a peculiar manner. He has been choked to death by an iron rod in his gullet. That too very near our house. I shudder to think of the danger that you and the baby were exposed to last night."

Parvati burst into tears. In between her sobs, she narrated the incidents of the previous night. He stroked her head thoughtfully. What a brave woman! He had never thought that she had it in her to act so purposefully. She deserved an award from the Government. But no!! She may be imprisoned for killing a tiger. The government protected tigers. So it was tantamount to destroying government's property.

"Paro, you are not to breathe a word about last night's incident to anyone. Not to anyone, you understand, not even to Lakshmi. If word gets around you will have to go to jail."

Parvati looked fearfully at her husband. She nodded as she wiped her tears. Parvati went about her daily chores listlessly. She could not wash away the sense of guilt in her mind.

Often in her baby's cry she hears the tiger's painful roar again.

The Meek Shall Inherit

Savitri

Savitri pressed her cheek tightly as tears welled up in her eyes. It seemed as if her mother-in-law's malevolent eyes would pierce into her.

"You think you are beautiful, don't you? Your beauty is as good as cow dung in my house."

Savitri removed her palm and saw two dark welts on her cheek where her mother-in-law had scratched her. Her mother-in-law tittered—"Now your fair cheeks are scarred for life. You can pride yourself on your scarred cheeks." She went away cackling to herself.

Savitri looked at the mirror and saw a slim figure. Everyone considered her beautiful, though she herself had hardly spared much thought on her beauty. But the slim waist, the rippling dark hair framing a golden complexion, the dark kohl lined eyes and a rosebud mouth invited many thoughts in many minds. Little wonder then, that marriage proposals poured in when she became eighteen. It was her uncle, her father's youngest brother who had cared for her when she was orphaned at the age of five. While nurturing the little orphan girl, he had left his youth behind. With great care he had sifted through the proposals and zeroed down on Ramaswamy Iyer, the only son of a widowed mother. He was well endowed with property, but that didn't stop him from accepting all the cash and jewellery that Savitri brought with her. His widowed mother had insisted that her uncle should gift some of his large property to her son as a wedding gift. After all he was a bachelor with nobody to give away anything to. Savitri's uncle, Krishna Iyer had not done so. Somewhere in the deepest recesses of his mind, he was perhaps apprehensive of the future of his tender niece.

Savitri looked up to see her husband creeping in. He came near her and cleared his throat apologetically.

"Amma has a bad temper, don't mind her. As a widow she has suffered so much, you see…"

"So now I must suffer like her! What logic is this?" retorted Savitri, the throbbing cheek quivering her voice. Ramaswamy brought cotton dipped in antiseptic lotion and bathed her cheek tenderly. He soothed his wife only to scurry away downstairs when he heard his mother's stentorian call. Savitri sighed. She had to face the fact that her husband was a weakling, a coward, a wimp. He was gentle, and he loved and admired her. But no emotion was strong enough to withstand his fear of his mother. It was not just the fear of a dutiful son, but the all-encompassing fear of a weak person in the face of superior strength. Savitri often felt that her husband behaved as if he was hypnotised by his mother. He knew that she was cruel, jealous, and greedy. But years of toeing the line was a habit hard to break, provided he even wanted to break it. Her mother-in-law discouraged visits by Savitri's uncle. When he did, it was like a prison visit under the grim eyes of the jailor.

Savitri wept copiously thinking of the horrible turn her life had taken. From a petted and pampered darling she was now reduced to taunted and tortured victim. She was reviled by her mother-in-law and her husband had neither the guts nor the inclination to stand up for her. Even sleeping with her was at the whim of his mother. She rationed out sex too, so that Ramaswamy would not get too attached to his wife. A strong survival streak in her impelled her to control her son. After all she was a widow and all the ancestral property belonged to her son. Patriarchy often showed its most ugly face through women. Slowly the control freak in her became a juggernaut, trampling and terrorising all in the vicinity, particularly her tender daughter-in-law. The more beauteous Savitri was victimised, the more powerful became the control freak in the old lady.

Till one day all bonds broke down for Savitri.

She was locked up in the upstairs room, while her mother-in-law and husband attended a wedding. Savitri looked out of the window and saw the cowherd boy sauntering in the courtyard.

"Muthu, can you help a suffering woman?"

Muthu came running up to the window. Savitri had often given him rice gruel and pickles on the sly when her mother-in-law was away from the kitchen. Savitri scribbled a letter to her uncle and threw it down to the boy along with her ring. It took her some time to explain to him the directions to her uncle's village a few miles away. She pleaded with Muthu to go as fast as possible, promising him a big feast and a reward at the end of his journey. It was two months since her marriage. She hoped her uncle would be back from overseeing his various estates. Two days later, her uncle arrived unannounced. Marks on Savitri's arms and face and her glazed eyes told him more than her short letter. Silently he waited while she packed. Her mother-in-law raved and ranted while her husband blubbered. Just as they reached the doorway, Savitri's uncle turned and with all the might of pent up rage, gave Ramaswamy Iyer a slap across the face. When Savitri looked back, tears were coursing down his cheeks whether out of pain of the slap or her departure, she did not know.

†

It took Savitri several months to recover from the memories of hell. To her utter dismay she found she was carrying Ramaswamy's child. But her dismay was short lived. Motherhood gave her a hitherto absent determination. When the child was born, she made a resolve.

"Chittappa, I want to file a case asking for a share of my husband's property for my son."

Her uncle was aghast. A woman fighting for property of her estranged husband was unheard of in that small district.

"Savitri, we have enough money for you and your son. After all, everything I have is yours."

"No, Chittappa, my son should get the share that is rightfully his." Savitri was adamant in the face of her uncle's arguments.

The case was filed and dragged on for two years. Ramaswamy Iyer did try to sneak into Savitri's house in the hope of seeing his son. But he was unceremoniously sent away by Savitri's uncle. Her husband's timidity filled Savitri with contempt.

Savitri could never forget that day in court when both her uncle and she were waiting for the judge. Ramaswamy tried to catch her eye when his mother was not looking. But Savitri studiously avoided looking at him. The only time she looked at him was when his lawyers in the course of the argument stated that the child was not fathered by Ramaswamy Iyer but by Savitri's uncle. She looked at her husband with venomous revulsion. From the corner of her eye she could see her mother-in-law's gloating face. After the uproar the court was adjourned. At the next hearing the child was produced. Savitri took care to dress her son in the same silk dhoti as his father. She even smeared his forehead with sandalwood paste like Ramaswamy. The judge took one look at the child and at the larger version standing in front of him and immediately stated that there was not an iota of doubt on the parentage of the child. Half of Ramaswamy's property was made over to a trust in the child's name. Savitri was one of the trustees along with her uncle. Thus ended the saga of Savitri's marriage. Or did it?

Savitri built a huge house right opposite her mother-in-law's domain and lived there in regal splendour. Dressed in the best of Kanjeevaram saris, with diamonds glistening on her ears and nose, she would swing on the veranda all the time keenly aware of her mother-in-law's baleful looks and her husband's love lorn glances. When Savitri's uncle died she allowed Ramaswamy to come into her home and life…to fulfil her physical needs, much to his mother's ire. But the old lady was now a paper tiger. Ramaswamy Iyer changed one master for another. For Savitri only used him but never loved him. Perhaps that was the price he paid for never becoming a real man. His manhood was only for Savitri's use.

As for Savitri, she was enjoying her control over a man.

Thumbing my Nose

Rooprani

Rooprani plucked the offending grey hair from her temples, frowning in concentration. She looked in the mirror for more silver strands. With precision, she ruthlessly pulled them from their roots. Her vigilant eyes moved to her face, dreading a wrinkle. She sighed with relief as she touched her firm and glowing skin. Twenty-five years of marriage and nine children had not played havoc with Rooprani's body. She was remarkably well preserved for a 40-year-old woman. "But I am 40 years young", thought Rooprani who felt as vigorous and lively as she was at 20. Life was good to her. A husband who was besotted with her, a flourishing cloth business in Lahore's prosperous Anarkali Bazaar, six strapping sons and three demure daughters, and three obedient daughters-in-law...Rooprani's cup was indeed full.

Yet a faint disquiet tormented her.

"Bharat chhod do. Angrez wapas jao"(Quit India, English go back). Rooprani ran to the terrace to get a clear view of the procession of protestors on the road. She could see young men with a sprinkling of women in home-spun khaddar shouting slogans and punching the air. The noise and the fist-raised salutes jostled the peace in the mohalla. The police stood by watching the protesters derisively, ready to rain blows at a single barked order. Rooprani watched with her heart in her mouth. She scanned the procession, hoping that her sons were not among the protesters.

However, her two eldest sons were holding placards, defiantly shouting the slogans, *"Angrezi sarkar hai, hai"* (Down with the British Government). Rooprani watched them, silently praying that they would avoid slogans on the British monarch. That would definitely invite a *lathi* charge. The protesters moved out of sight and Rooprani slowly climbed down the stairs.

Ever since Mahatma Gandhi had called off the Quit India movement, Lahore had periodically erupted into protest marches and rallies against the British rule of the Indian subcontinent. Added to this was the tension between Hindus and Muslims with Jinnah calling for a separate nation for Muslims. Her three eldest sons had joined the Hindu Mahasabha, in an endeavour to protect Hindu interests. Rooprani knew they were playing with fire. But her remonstration was in vain. She knew that the police kept a watch on their home, waiting for the first opportunity when her sons would overstep the line. Once they were arrested, their futures were doomed, by a long round of police stations, courts and prison.

"Suppose they are sent off to *kaala pani?*" Rooprani shuddered as she pictured the dreaded jail in the Andamans. She could never communicate her fears effectively to her sons. Now that they were members of the aggressive Hindu Mahasabha, their Muslim neighbours, particularly the men were a trifle wary of them. Rooprani lived in the dread of some neighbour passing on information to the British intelligence. In the times they were living, even innocuous information could be used to charge a man with treason.

†

That night Rooprani waited till all the men had been served their dinner, before reiterating her fears. Looking at her husband, she asked—

"Have you no authority over your sons, or are you blind to the danger they are inviting?"

"Oh ho Roop! What fresh trouble are you thinking of?"

"Your sons are now at loggerheads with the sarkar. You know what that means?"

"That is no sarkar of ours. We will be ruled by Indians only", growled Deshraj, Rooprani's eldest son.

"We will be ruled by Indian Hindus only." piped in Mulkhraj.

"Hush, our Muslim neighbours will misinterpret your rash statements".

"Let them. I am not afraid of anyone."

Rooprani looked at her sons with derision. "If you want to play with your lives, then feel free to do so. But you had no business to marry and drag your wives into this definite misery."

"Chaijee, if every freedom fighter thought in a similar manner, then they would be sitting at home, watching India go to the dogs."

"To the English dogs."

Deshraj's wife quickly closed the windows. The argument continued late into the night. Rooprani wanted to scream in frustration. Her husband was too gentle to assert his authority over her hot-headed sons. The sons were too inspired by the impressive orators in the Hindu Mahasabha, to heed Rooprani's counsel. They laughed at her fears and gently taunted her for being a *darpoke.*

†

"Rooprani, Roopraniiii, where are you? Hurry, your sons are in danger. The police are on their way!"

Rooprani ran down with turmeric stained hands. Her neighbour Kamla was outside the door, literally hopping on one foot in impatience.

"Hurry, Rooprani. My youngest son saw a bunch of policemen on the main road. They were talking about your house. Perhaps they are coming here to search for something or someone. Your sons are…." Kamla trailed off. Both women looked at each other and understood without words, the danger looming over their heads. Rooprani thought in desperation.

Were there any incriminating books or posters in the house? Thank God all the men were in the shop. Or were they? Good Lord, those swords and daggers were in Deshraj's bedroom! They had been distributed at the last meeting. *Hai Ram,* what was the law? Knives and daggers with a blade more than six inches were banned? Or was it four inches?

"Roop, there is no time to think. Do something", Kamla urged impatiently.

"Kamla, ask the mohalla sarpanch to lock the gate. Unlock it slowly after asking many questions. Play for time." Kamla ran off.

Rooprani rushed upstairs and opened the window in Deshraj's bedroom. The window overlooked the narrow street. Right opposite was the window of Kamla's house. Rooprani remembered how the boys would walk across the street daringly on a wooden plank placed between the windows. She called out to her daughter-in-law.

"Sumitra, take out all the swords and knives that your foolish husband has hidden away. Hurry!"

Across the street Rooprani called out to Kamla's daughter across the street. "Preeto, spread the quilts close to your window. Sumitra will throw the knives through this window. There will be no sound if they fall on the quilt. Be careful *beta*. You can save your brothers. Rooprani turned to her daughter-in-law. "Sumitra throw the dangerous things carefully. Do it when the police are not looking. If anything falls into the street below, we are all doomed. If you find anything else that is dangerous, don't hesitate. Just throw it across."

Rooprani looked at her other daughters and daughters-in-law. "Why are you all crowding here? Go about your daily jobs as if nothing is happening. Be natural. One of you stay back to help Sumitra. And no drama or tears. We will come out of this danger, never fear."

Rooprani's confidence was infectious. The women wiped their tears and fears and went about their daily chores while waiting for the dreaded sound of the boots. Rooprani had a precious few seconds to instruct Preeto and Sumitra. "When you feel that you have removed all dangerous things then slowly come down the stairs. I'll understand."

†

Rooprani went down the stairs to the main doorway of the house. She sat down on the threshold, and the six policemen came marching down the mohalla. Everybody was out on the street. Many women were looking out of the windows. There was dread and fear in every face. What would the events bring to the street? Would these young men be taken away to prison only to come back beaten and broken? Rooprani kept sitting nonchalantly while her mind raced. Thank God, there was no English officer with the policemen. Somehow she felt that it would be easier to deal with Indian policemen. She looked at them; some of them were young boys who donned the air of authority consciously. They looked every bit determined to do their duty at any cost. The older ones looked a bit uneasy, uncomfortable, walking into Indian homes and dragging out their fellow countrymen.

Rooprani looked for the most uncomfortable expression and decided to make him her target. She recognised one of the boys as Shakuntala's son. He lived on the other side of Anarkali Bazaar with his mother. Rooprani remembered Shakuntala's pride when he was selected as a constable. Wonder if she will feel the same pride now, thought Rooprani. From the corner of her eye Rooprani saw Veer Singh, her servant edging to slowly slink away and warn his masters at the shop.

"Stop," hissed Rooprani. "Don't you dare drag your masters here. I will not involve them in this." Veer Singh looked doubtful. But he dared not provoke Rooprani's ire.

"We have a warrant to search the house of Deshraj and Mulkhraj Khanna"

On hearing this, Rooprani sat down more comfortably covering the entire threshold.

"Search warrant?" she echoed. "Search warrant for what? My sons are businessmen. What does the sarkar want to search our house for?"

"We have information that they are hoarding dangerous weapons in the house. This is against the law. Let us do our duty."The senior police constable cleared his throat a couple of times. Rooprani instinctively felt that he was not too convinced of his 'duty'.

"Dangerous weapons? That is right. We have a meat cleaver in the backyard. Perhaps you are looking for that."

"We also have the vegetable slicer and the pounding sticks for spices." People were sniggering.

"Perhaps the police are going to cook in the *thana*."

The policemen were very uncomfortable. When they went to execute a search warrant, most people either grovelled at their feet or stood aside defiantly. Nobody reduced the whole operation into a joke as this woman was doing. There was an enigmatic quality about her, which while not being overtly assertive, was very clear that no aggression would be brooked.

Rooprani's ears were glued to the window upstairs. She could hear faint thuds and started talking loudly to cover the suspicious sounds. "We are only women here. Our men are at work. How can we allow you to search the house? I don't even know what is written in the paper."

"We will read it out to you". The police was relieved that only a small formality stood between him and his duty. He quickly read out the search warrant. Rooprani pretended to listen, while all the time she was concentrating on the sounds from upstairs. Why was Sumitra not coming down? Had they removed all the offending articles? How much longer could she ward the police off?

"This is my house. This space is sacred to me and my family. I can't allow you to enter my home, warrant or no warrant." The police were aghast. Nobody had refused them point blank before. They had no orders to deal with defiant women. They could not offer violence to this woman. The whole mohalla would turn against them in a minute, and their retreat would be cut off once the main gates were closed. They looked at Rooprani, visibly perplexed.

"You can't stop us from doing our duty. If need be we will force our way in.", the senior constable said with a hint of a threat.

"Force your way in? *Hai Ram!* This is what your mother taught you? Force your way into innocent Hindu homes and insult the womenfolk!"

"But *behenji,* we have not insulted you!"

"Wanting to enter a home when the men are not here, is insult enough. I have my daughters and daughters-in-law in the house."

"We can send for your husband. We are willing to wait." The senior constable was confident that no one could escape with the weapons from the front door. He had posted a constable at the back door. Rooprani was not at all happy with this assurance. She did not want the men to be in the house, as this would only precipitate matters. Her sons in their aggression would just invite trouble in a foolhardy manner. As long as she played the role of an indecisive helpless woman, she could buy time.

"Oh well, if you have to enter, then I can't stop you. You will have to step over me. And don't you dare touch me to remove me from the threshold."

The police looked at one another. Step over this virago? No way. As men they did not dare touch her in front of the whole mohalla. The women police had not accompanied the posse. The senior constable could sense the animosity of the watching crowd. He had no intention of offering explanations to his irate boss, if things got out of hand. He looked at Rooprani, wondering at her temerity in defying the police. Most women he knew cowered in terrified fear, when they saw the policemen. Here was a Jhansi ki rani hell bent on making him and his men look like fools. He could hear suppressed sniggers already. He tried to reason it out with Rooprani. She stood her ground. With each passing moment, she became more defiant.

"You are Shakuntala's son aren't you? When you step over me remember my friend, your mother. Don't forget to say my *namaste* to her. She will be proud of her son's exploits," Rooprani taunted. Shakuntala's son squirmed in embarrassment. Rooprani pressed home her advantage.

She looked at the Muslim constable. "And you *beta,* if your Ammi was here, would you also step over her to do your duty?" Rooprani kept berating the constables, goading them into taking one wrong step

From the corner of her eye she saw the senior constable whispering to his subaltern. The young constable quickly went. Rooprani was sure that he had gone to get further orders or to fetch policewomen. There were only a few policewomen in Lahore. So Rooprani knew that getting them over would take time. But she knew that if senior officers came to the scene, they would not hesitate to bodily remove her to prison for obstructing the police's work. If a *gora* officer came then there would be no leniency. Rooprani's thoughts raced. She would have to keep the police at bay till Sumitra came down from upstairs. Suddenly she saw Kamla's daughter Preeto in the small crowd congregated near her house.

"*Hai* Preeto, call your mother to come and see my plight. I am a woman of a rich businessman and here I am being insulted and threatened by policemen young enough to be my sons."

The young policeman tried to protest, but his senior shut him down. The senior constable was intrigued by Rooprani's behaviour. If there were weapons in the house, then this battle axe of a woman should be wary of taking the police on. But if there were weapons, then why was she indulging in histrionics? Nobody could get out of or into the house, so no help was forthcoming. Yet the drama was going on. Was she buying time? For what? Even if she hid the weapons, the police would ferret them out!

Preeto said loudly, "Roop *masi,* Amma is folding all the quilts. But I will call her."

Rooprani thought, 'Oh ho, the quilts are being folded. That means all the weapons have gone across the street.' She looked towards the staircase casually and saw Sumitra coming down slowly.

"Sumitra, come here, these policemen want to search the house for weapons that your husband and brother-in-law have kept inside the house."

"Weapons, what weapons. We have nothing in the house. But Chaijee, if the police want to search, let them do their duty. After all they are only following orders."

"You think I should let them in? If you say so I will. I was just trying to stop them from entering a house where no menfolk are present at the moment."

The senior policeman was perplexed to see Rooprani capitulate. "Äll right. You are like my sons. Why should I make your life difficult? After all you have been sent by other officers who were too cowardly to come themselves and sent you to face the music."

†

The police needed no further indication. They barged in after showing the search warrant to the mohalla sarpanch. They went through all the rooms of the huge haveli with a fine-toothed comb. Nothing even remotely connected to a weapon was found. All the windows were opening into the street. Nobody could have jumped out, since the police were keeping watch downstairs. Nothing could have been thrown out either, since the sound would have alerted the police. The senior constable looked at the window and across the street to Kamla's house and wondered where the weapons were! After all our information cannot be wrong, he thought to himself. But where had they hidden it?

After a thorough search, they came downstairs empty handed. Rooprani handed them big brass glasses of freshly made sherbet.

"Searching a big house is hard work, particularly when there is nothing to show for it", Rooprani said gently. Now that the danger had been averted, she could afford to be generous to the enemy.

That night, Rooprani raved, ranted, pleaded and finally won the day. Her two eldest sons were sent off to Mussoorie to start a new business.

From that day onwards, Rooprani was called Jhansi Rani by everyone in the mohalla.

The Professional Palmist

Ambika

On the steps of the Chottanikkara temple in Kerala, she waylaid me with the persevering persistence of an insurance agent. Ambika must have had the perceptive insight to discern that I abhorred the word "No". So she followed me to sanctum sanctorum showing me all the scribblings on dog eared pieces of paper. She showed pictures of various palms; fat, thin, shapely, crooked, all with the mandatory lines delineated in ink. Ambika was a palmist, a 'professional palmist and astrologer', as she called herself. Her emphasis on the word 'professional' automatically consigned all others in the temple premises to the rubbish heap.

Ambika was waiting for me when I came out of the temple. In the face of superior energy, I had to give in. In fact I found it less tiring to agree to Ambika than resist her. She gesticulated towards a corner near some bushes. I followed her, my urban upbringing making me suspicious, as I looked apprehensively around. Ambika interpreted my apprehension.

"Don't worry Chechi, I am not a common thief. When the Goddess has given me such a storehouse of knowledge, why would I resort to low-down thieving?" She held my palm and muttered a prayer accompanied by some tantric gestures with her fingers. All calculated to impress, no doubt. For a long time she peered over my palm, pinching it here and stretching it there. I felt quite silly standing there. The passers-by goggled at me, some sniggering to note that a victim had been caught. All the while Ambika kept talking, her garrulousness rooting me down.

"Why Chechi, you are showered with the grace of the Devi. You don't have to work for a living at all." Fingers relentlessly caressing the computer key board trying to churn out 'pieces' for fussy publishers was obviously no 'hard work' in Ambika's comprehension. My manicured fingers precluded manual work which was really hard work for Ambika.

"Ah! I see a loving husband. But he does not appreciate you enough."

Now this was a clever gambit. Most wives, I suppose feel that they deserve more appreciation for their visible and non-visible efforts to keep a marriage going. With this observation, most women softened their suspicious stance. So did I and Ambika was quick to press home the advantage.

"You're the pillar of strength in your home. It is because of you that all relationships are maintained."

Like most women, I prided myself on my imagined indispensability to my home and family. Ambika sensed that I was warming towards her.

"You have creative talent."

"Yes, I write." The words were out before I could stop them, thus unwittingly giving Ambika a further opening.

"I see great fame. I see money pouring in." Ambika was obviously unaware that very few writers in India could earn their bread butter and jam through writing. However it felt good to know that name and fame were awaiting me at the next corner. Perhaps I would win the Booker prize. Or Hollywood would buy the screen rights of my novel for an obscenely large amount of money. Ambika wanted me to have my cake and eat it too, so who was I to complain.

"Your husband will always support you." Yes of course. A hard working spouse was the best ticket to survival for a writer. Ambika rattled on in this fashion for a quarter of an hour, saying much, yet revealing nothing new or earth shattering. I parted with a hundred rupee note at the end of this session. Ambika demanded two hundred rupees. I was regretfully thinking I should have given fifty rupees. However despite this difference in viewpoints, we parted amicably.

†

I observed Ambika for almost a week, since I was residing in the temple guest house. My interest in her could have been triggered by the news that my agents had negotiated a successful deal with the publishers. It could be coincidence. But a struggling writer like me was willing to clutch on to any lucky mascot. Ambika's modus operandi was simple. Like an intelligence agent, she observed, assimilated and stored away any scrap of information, to be reproduced again at appropriate moments. She stationed herself at the temple parking lot and observed the pilgrims as they streamed in. Once she had zeroed in on her victims, she subjected them to an eagle eyed scrutiny, catching onto any information that she could glean.

"Your husband takes great care of you", she told a well dressed woman. Earlier on Ambika had observed the woman's husband opening the car door for her and helping her over the innumerable steps. To a woman walking slowly behind her husband and chattering children she said—"You care for your family much more than they care for you," thus pandering to the whims of her client's self-pity. Ambika observed clothes, jewellery, the softness of the palms, and the devout expressions on the faces. From each detail, she squeezed out her conclusion with the triumphant air of a magician producing a rabbit out of the hat. Most of the times she was right. When she was wrong, she covered up with the ease of a hardened door to door salesman. Ambika did not have a degree in gender psychology. But she knew that a lot could be understood from the gait of a woman—her confidence level, low self-esteem, her aggression, her happiness etc.

Ambika was a happy professional palmist. She rarely predicted catastrophes. If she predicted illness, she was quick to point out that it was short-lived. If she read financial disaster in the palm, she gave a prayer that would ward off the disaster. After all prayers can never go wrong, was her conclusion. Marital happiness was very high on her list of predictions. Unhappy wives were given the hope that the 'bad period' was over and marital felicity awaited them. Erring husbands could be brought to the fold by a short prayer repeated 108 times. The prayer was potent in its assured success. Those awaiting marriage were told that the wait was worthwhile since a 'very good husband' was seen in the palm. She rarely talked about the trauma of betrayal and almost never about death. Most of

Ambika's clients went away happy. It paid Ambika well for her to tell her clients that God was in the Heaven and all was well with their world or at least it would be shortly.

Ambika treated her job with a reverence that was almost amusing if she herself was not so serious about it. She did not for even a second feel that she was cheating people with a whole lot of mumbo jumbo. "People come to the temple to tell Devi their troubles and seek solutions. I just help them and tell them that things will soon be better. That is not cheating." Her arguments seemed logical to me. To me Ambika seemed pretty much empowered. Her gaiety was infectious. And this gaiety had very little to sustain it, as I soon learnt.

Unknowingly and certainly unintentionally, I got more interested in Ambika. Since I spent almost the whole day in the temple premises, I had all the time in the world to serve my interest. Once she had told my future, Ambika's interest in me as a customer waned. Sitting on the temple steps, in between her various clients, I learnt that she was the sole bread winner for her family for the time being. Her husband having worked for many back breaking hours rolling *beedi*s had succumbed to tuberculosis. He had been advised total rest. For the last one year, Ambika had held the body and soul of her family together. In Chottanikkara the sanctum sanctorum opened at dawn, for pilgrims to get a glimpse of the goddess.

Ambika woke up at the crack of dawn to clean, wash and cook for her family and keep her husband's medicines and special diet ready. Then she went to clean an office nearby, before rushing off to the temple. When the temple closed between noon and evening, she worked in a pharmacy. Then again back to being a professional palmist. Finally when she reached home it was seven or eight at night, after finishing the shopping for home. Ambika was holding three jobs. She was also a wife and mother. But all her roles she fulfilled with aplomb. She lived all her roles, but she was especially fond of being a 'professional palmist'. After giving furtive glances here and there, she whispered to me that 50 per cent of her earnings from the temple, she kept aside to buy a house that she had earmarked near the temple. She had already saved half the needed amount.

"I'll soon get the rest, Chechi. I am sure by the grace of the Devi."

I almost reached for my purse to add to her savings, but something in the straight backed gait held me back.

†

I visited Chottanikkara a year later. When climbing the steps of the temple I was eager to see the goddess and Ambika. I saw the Devi in her usual place in the sanctum sanctorum, but Ambika was not at her usual point in the parking lot. I finally saw her holding forth with her hapless victim. She seemed to have aged disproportionately, I thought. But the vigour seemed undimmed, or was it? But the perseverance was still there one hundred per cent. A bright smile lit her face as she spotted me. Sitting on our favourite steps we updated each other. She listened eagerly, as I recounted the success of my book and the new deadline that I was working on. She felt that she owned some part of the success since she had predicted it. There was silence when I asked for her news. With a deadpan face, she told me that her husband had run away with a girl from the dispensary where he went to get his medicines. He had taken all their savings. With one stroke, he had destroyed her home and all the dreams for a house. There had been no news from him. Some said that he was at Salem, working in a shop. Some saw him at Kanya Kumari, rowing a ferry boat.

"But Chechi, it does not matter, where he is. I have put him away from my mind."

Ambika still had three jobs, but had only one role of a mother to fulfil. The distant dream of buying a house still flickered bright.

"I have started saving again. That house got sold. But I'll soon find another one." Ambika exuded a rare confidence that belied her circumstances.

"How come you didn't predict your husband's betrayal?" The question was out even before I could stop it.

Ambika looked at me steadily.

"Chechi, I don't go around reading my palm or my worthless husband's. What money can I earn from wasting my time like that?"

Her answer seemed quite logical to me. She was back to being a professional palmist. But to me it seemed that a thread of betrayal, lost trust, separation, sorrow dominated her predictions. But that was life she told her clients. "And I have a prayer that will ward off everything. Guaranteed success."

As I was leaving the temple, that evening, I gave Ambika five thousand rupees. "This is for predicting the success of my book."

Ambika firmly gave the money back.

"No Chechi. If you had given me the money before I told you my story, I would have still kept it. Now I am not sure whether you're giving it to me, because I am a good professional palmist, or an unfortunate woman."

I respected Ambika's self-esteem. When I turned to look at her, she was on the temple steps, holding tightly the palm of her next customer.

She Found her Voice

Narsamma

"You bitch, will you kill me by starving me?"

Narsamma stirred the rice pot again nonchalantly. She had heard these abuses from the time she was married sixteen years ago. The tirade went on, even as she blew into the smoking mud stove. She did not know what was worse, his constant yelling or her painful watering eyes. Narsamma knew from the level of shouting that her husband had imbibed quite freely of the locally produced liquor. She wondered how he managed to fund his drinking, since there was no money in the house. She thought that he must have worked as a labourer at the bus depot loading and unloading the buses.

Bastard! He blows his money on the useless liquor which within a few hours he will excrete as urine. But he cannot buy some vegetables to feed the hungry children! Narsamma fumed quietly, keeping her thoughts to herself behind a facade of docility. That is how she had survived his abuses, blows and kicks and rapes. By just keeping silent. She had never ever opened her mouth, even when he had kicked her in the stomach and she had bled the fetus out. She had watched dumbly as he had sold all the brass plates and glasses her parents had given her, to fund his liquor. She had never screamed in frustration that she had to scrounge to feed her three children on her meagre earnings as a farm worker.

Narsamma was always silent. Her husband raged more and more as her silence incensed him and goaded him to beat her more, merely for the satisfaction of hearing her yell in pain. Her silence was the weapon and her armour, but alas never did it protect her from the back breaking thrashings.

Narsamma quietly served the rice to the drunkard with salt and a green chilli. That was all there was for dinner. Her husband looked at the plate, at Narsamma and deliberately picked up the plate and threw it out of the hut. She looked at the splattered rice which the dogs were lapping up. But she only saw the rice for which she had pleaded and grovelled at the feet of the landlord of the farm she worked in. She only heard his stern voice which reminded her that she had already taken an advance on her wages. He also reminded her pitilessly that in her emaciated state she was not fit to work.

Why did he have to throw it? He could have left it. My children and I could have had a full stomach. Hardly had the thought left her mind when she felt a stinging blow on her face. Blood gushed from her lips even as he screamed, "You whore, whole day you are out and this is what you give me to eat?" He kicked her in the back, even as her children huddled in a corner wide eyed with fear. Narsamma bit her lips increasing her pain even more. As if her silence goaded him, he turned to the cowering children. Narsamma's husband dragged their fifteen-year-old daughter by the hair, screaming abuses at her all the while. "You daughter of a bitch, old enough to gorge on food but not old enough to work! Who do you think you are, a heroine? Go out. Spread your legs for some man and bring money home."

Through the mists of pain Narsamma heard these words. For a moment, everything was silent within her. Then she got up, and limped to the corner of the hut, picked up the pestle and with one well aimed blow she broke her husband's hand. He yelped in pain even as he left the shivering girl's hair. After that hell was let loose. Narsamma's husband writhed in pain, screamed expletives and with his good hand tried to grab Narsamma. Every time he came near, she whacked him with the pestle. With all the might of her hurt motherhood, she pushed him out of the hut and locked the door.

†

That night nobody slept in Narsamma's hut. Her husband screamed in pain, but his drinking cronies locked their doors. Narsamma's children were petrified of what the morning would bring. Narsamma herself was aghast at what she had done. She had always been told that her husband was her lord and master. What kind of a master is he that he only kicks and abuses? He does not bring a single rupee into the house and wants to be treated like a lord! Narsamma had been taught that men knew best. But what did he know best? To drink, beat and then stick his filthy manhood into me! She had been taught that as a woman she was always subservient to her husband. Why, just because he had some extra flesh between his legs? I earn, cook, clean and take care of the children. Yet I should be subservient? In the darkness of the night, Narsamma mulled over the darkness in her life. She realised that in the sixteen years she had never known a single day that was free of pain and carefree. She also understood that she had been silent because she had been taught to be silent. She had been taught to accept her fate. Are we taught to accept this lot as inevitable because our elders know that there is no escape? This fate is so inexorable that acceptance is the only way? Narsamma thought and thought for long. In those sixteen years, in the midst of all the drudgery and pain, she had never stopped to think why she had to suffer pain. But that night she questioned everything. She also understood that by breaking her husband's hand she had broken every tie, every adage that she had been taught, every tradition that she had grown up with. What use was tradition if it could not keep me from pain?

†

Next morning, her husband tried to push his way into the house, but Narsamma was waiting with the pestle.

"What do you think you are doing, you filthy carcass? Let me in. This is my house," screamed her husband.

"Why?" Narsamma shot back. "Have you built it? I built it from the brick and mud with my own hands. The tarpaulin on the roof is from what I begged from neighbours shamelessly. You don't give a single rupee to the house! How is it your house?"

Narsamma's husband was dumbstruck. He had always waited for a reaction from her when he beat her mercilessly. It seemed that she had him now in her merciless grip. Almost blind with the pain of his broken arm, he shrieked, abused, threatened and tried to push his way in, only to be thwacked hard on his legs. Hearing the commotion, neighbours gathered around the hut. Soon two gangs were formed, with most of the men in one group, vociferously blaming Narsamma for breaking her husband's hand. The other group – mostly of women – equally vociferously blamed Narsamma's husband for his brutal behaviour. When the groups were outshouting each other, Narsamma stood on a stool to make herself heard.

"Why is everyone shouting so that you can only hear your own voice and drown everyone else's? That is exactly what my husband has been doing for all these years. He screams so much that he could never hear my pain or the children's. He abused so much that he could never hear our hate for him. In his drunken stupor, he even forgets his relationships. Yes, I have broken his hand. Do you know why? He was pushing his daughter to become a whore so that she could give him money to drink."

A wave of revulsion rippled through the crowd with even the men looking at Narsamma's husband in disgust.

"He does not give money to buy food. But he buys his wretched drink. His children go to bed hungry, but he sleeps in drunkenness. He gives us nothing but abuses, kicks and thrashings. Then you all expect me to care for him?"

She struck a chord with every woman in the crowd who had a similar saga of pain, of a brutalised body and a mutilated self-esteem. There were sympathetic murmurs in the crowd.

"But Narsamma, you can't leave him out in the open. He has to come home."

"Why, so that he can beat us more. No. I don't want him and my children don't want him. If he steps inside the house, I will break his bones. I am not afraid of him anymore. He has nothing to give us. So why should I be afraid?"

A stalemate had been reached. Narsamma's husband was by this time blubbering in pain. Narsamma was adamant on not letting him in the house. "But Narsamma, your husband becomes such a monster only after he drinks." Devamma, Narsamma's neighbour said trying to defuse the situation. Narsamma turned towards her as another truth dawned on her.

"Yes Devamma, he is a bad man when he is in his senses, but he becomes a cruel monster when he is senseless with drink. Your husband becomes a thief when he is drunk. Didn't he steal two hundred rupees from your trunk, the money you had saved for your son's tuition?"

Devamma's husband tried to avoid the accusing glances and slunk away into the background.

"You Maniamma, you are so old, your hair is grey, yet your old man kicks you when you don't give him money for drinking. Neelu, Godavari, Dhanya, Ganga why are you all quiet? Every one of you has been beaten by your drunken husbands. Why do we put up with it? Because we are taught that our husbands are our gods. What kind of gods keep their children starving so that they can drink? Every one of us works eighteen hours a day to keep the fires in our stoves burning, while our men drink away their earnings and beat us and burden us with more mouths to feed." Many of the men tried to slink away unobtrusively. But Narsamma was on a rampage.

"My brothers, where are you going? To the liquor shop to drink away your shame? My sisters, drink is the devil that makes our husbands monsters, starves our children and destroys our homes. Let us destroy the drink." There was utter silence that greeted this bold announcement. Then the women started chattering together. So many questions, so many doubts, so many apprehensions. Narsamma got down from the stool, locked her house, gathered her children and shouted—

"I am going to destroy the devil. Who wants to come with me?"

She walked away purposefully, without looking back. Devamma ran to catch up with her. Soon the women followed her with the men following at a distance to see the outcome. By the time Narsamma reached the two liquor shops on the highway, the crowd had swelled to a hundred women. The news spread like wildfire that Narsamma was going to destroy the 'Devil'. The local NGO *garu* also came out of his tiny office to judge the action. Narsamma went into the liquor shop, even as the owner stood immobile in shock. She picked up a bottle and smashed it on the pavement stone. Then pandemonium broke out. The women barged in, destroying every bottle in sight. They overturned cauldrons of fermenting liquor, smashed glasses. Within a few minutes the liquor shop was struck by a tsunami of women, catalysed into action by the common pain. When there was nothing left to destroy, they stood still, looking at Narsamma for the next course of action. She realised in that split second that leadership had been thrust on her.

"Sisters, just destroying this shop will not destroy the devil. We have to ensure that the liquor shops don't come up in Bitragunta again. For that we will have to go on a *dharna*."

†

The local policeman had come hurriedly after frantic calls from the shop owners. He was goaded by the men, "Arrest them arrest them police *garu*". But the constable took one look at the angry women and decided against arresting hundred women. In any case the NGO activist had whispered information that the shops were on the state highway—illegally on government land.

The women returned home. Narsamma cooked a meal of rice gruel with a green chilly chutney and ate with her children. It was the best meal in all her sixteen years. Her husband tried to enter the house again but was thrust outside. He spent that night, as he would spend many nights, on the temple verandah. Over the next few nights frustrated men threw stones at Narsamma's house hoping to frighten her from her mission. But other women chased them away. Most of the men had to either walk or take a bus to the next village for a drink. When they came home, they were locked out of their homes. The liquor shop owners tried to rebuild their shops, but were frightened off by the strength of the women of Bitragunta, who picketed the shops. Narsamma led from the front sitting in every *dharna,* and headed every delegation that met the Block Development Officer and the local Sub Divisional Magistrate. She spoke from the heart on the abject lives of the women of Bitragunta. Each sentence resonated with sixteen years of pain and humiliation. Each statement reflected the pernicious flow of liquor which had washed away any semblance of humanity in their lives. She even spoke to the newspaper man much to the amazement of her anti liquor friends.

A few days later, the NGO *garu* came to her hut to talk to her. Narsamma, quickly spread out the rather tattered mat on the cot and stood aside with her hands folded in respect. Many of her picketing friends came running leaving their chores.

"Narsamma, you have created a storm in the village, you know. The district collector has ensured that the liquor shops will not reopen." Narsamma stood twisting the edge of her sari, unsure on how to respond.

"Have you heard of Dubaghunta Rosamma. She too like you led a protest against liquor and it became such a movement that the 'Sarkar' was forced to close all liquor shops in the state of Andhra Pradesh. Do you want to lead a movement like Rosamma again?" asked the NGO *garu,* seeing for himself a role in the public limelight as Narsamma's mentor.

Narsamma was quick to answer. "No *Ayyagaru.* I am only a poor woman. I only know that I cannot take pain anymore. I am happy if in this village there are no liquor shops, I am happy if my sisters are not beaten and bruised for money."

Narsamma's friends protested loud against her refusal of a public role. NGO *garu* was disappointed. He was convinced that the scrawny Narsamma with her pain lined face and shabby clothes was just the right face for the anti-liquor movement. But she was adamant. As the NGO *garu* was leaving Narsamma asked, "Ayyagaru, if Rosamma had got the Sarkar to stop sale of liquor in the whole of Andhra Pradesh, how come it is still available?"

Smiling at her palpable ignorance he said "The Sarkar needs money. They get it from the sale of liquor."

"So, the Sarkar allows us to be beaten so that they can make money?" NGO *garu* was silent.

"Tell me *Ayyagaru,* what then is the difference between the Sarkar and my husband? One beats me and one allows me to be beaten."

Narsamma had certainly found her voice.

To be Human

Dulhan Begum

She was aptly named Dulhan Begum. With her roses and milk complexion, well etched features and her bright clothes she always glowed like a new bride. But it was her sunny view of the world that made her a ray of sunshine for her adoring family. Her presence enlivened any room and enriched every gathering. But the beautiful face masked a steely determination, which her family knew well never to challenge. She was never known to mince words, or compromise by an iota when it came to the well-being of her family, near and extended. That is what made her the centre of every family gathering and the 'go to' person in every crisis. Life really could not have been better for her.

But that morning creases marred her marble-like forehead as she folded her precious pashmina shawls. Winter was around the corner and as every year in Kashmir, it promised to be a long and hard winter. But it was not the chilly winds that dented Dulhan Begum's tranquility. It was the heat of the impending conflict between the two new nations that was worrying her. India and Pakistan, erstwhile colonies of the British Empire were now independent. But the Maharajah of Kashmir had neither acceded to India nor to Pakistan. The fluid situation was taking its toll on the Kashmiris. As per the Interim Agreement which Pakistan signed and India did not, Kashmir was to have a modicum of governance pending the final decision on the status of the landlocked region. Food and transport were the responsibilities of Pakistan. In the hope of squeezing the Kashmiri governance into acceding to India, Pakistan was withholding essential commodities, particularly salt. Literally Pakistan was holding a salt gun to the Kashmiri head. Dulhan Begum had started rationing salt for her family. For a Kashmiri family used to drinking salted tea, this was indeed a hardship. Her sons were in the militia, a fledgling army mandated to support the Maharajah's army in the endeavour to keep Pakistan from embarking on a military misadventure to wrest Kashmir. Life did not look too good.

"Ammi Jaan, Ammi Jaan, where are you?" Dulhan Begum quickly closed the wooden chest and came hurriedly out into the *baithak*.

"Ammi Jaan, tribal raiders from Pakistan have entered Kashmir through Muzzafarabad. They have killed Dhunichand Mehta, the Wazir Wazarat of Muzzafarabad point blank. They looted his house and burnt it down."

"What about his family?" Dulhan Begum asked with a dry throat.

"Nobody knows whether they have been killed or burnt in the house or have been abducted."

Dulhan Begum sat down heavily as if the weight of the tragedy was too much to bear. She remembered Dhunichand Mehta and his charming wife Krishna. She had met them at a common friend's wedding and was struck by the grace of the couple. She remembered clearly chatting about their respective families. Dulhan Begum's heart shuddered with horror at the fate that could have befallen the family. From that day onwards, each day brought spine-chilling news of human depravity. Hindu families were destroyed and their women abducted to face the brutal raiders. Anyone supporting the Hindu families or resisting the raiders was shot or tortured horribly. In Baramulla, even the missionary hospital and the nuns was not spared from the looting, carnage and rape that the raiders left in their wake. In Baramulla, a brave shopkeeper Maqbool Sherwani was tortured and killed since he was suspected of passing on information on the movements of the raiders, to the Maharajah's army and Hindu families. While Kashmir waited in agony the raiders were advancing slowly but steadily. The Maharajah and the Indian government quibbled on technicalities of a bail-out mission as innocent Kashmiris – both Hindus and Muslims – suffered unspeakable agonies.

Dulhan Begum stood in the kitchen supervising the making of *kahwa* for the mohalla committees. Every street had a committee which kept guard throughout the night, so as to warn the residents of a possible attack by the raiders. With only a few guns between them and even fewer men who could shoot straight, they were not adequately armed to fight off the ferocious raiders. But what they lacked in arms they made up with the irrevocable determination to ensure the safety of the residents. As the steaming samovars were handed over to the men, Dulhan Begum heard snatches of the conversation.

"We must be particularly careful that Hindu families are not targeted."

"How can we do that? They just come like locusts and destroy everything in sight."

"But in protecting the Hindus, every one of us can become targets."

After the declaration of independence on 15 August 1947 and the drawing up of the borders between India and Pakistan, North India and Eastern India had erupted into a communal bloodbath, with Muslims and Hindus killing each other in a frenzy of hate. The frustration of becoming non-citizens after living for centuries in a particular village or city, the agony of pulling out roots of generations and the helpless fear of having to leave the familiar and embark on a new journey found its expression in the most horrifying of human depravities. Hindus and Muslims massacred one another, only because the other was 'different' and belonged to another nation. Dulhan Begum's heart swelled with pride as she thought of Kashmir, the only haven in North India where communal riots had not erupted despite the mix of Hindu and Muslim populations. But the raiders have given us our share of agony, thought Dulhan Begum despondently.

†

Next morning brought more depressing news. The raiders had reached Shalteng, a few kilometers from Srinagar. The capital city was destined to fall, within a few hours to catastrophic destruction. Dulhan Begum was in a predicament. Her two sons were in the militia, far away at the borders. Her youngest son was stuck in Rawalpindi in Pakistan where he was studying medicine with no way of reaching India in the violent times they were living in. She and her daughters lived in Durgjan with the extended family of cousins, aunts and nephews who had taken shelter. But she was determined to protect her family, particularly the women. She shuddered as she imagined crude brutal hands on her delicate girls. She pushed the unwelcome thought away as she supervised the cleaning of the attic. She had decided that the women folk would hide there. In the event of the house being burnt down, they could jump to the neighbouring roof and run away or.... Dulhan Begum could not even think of the alternative.

That evening her daughter brought even more disquieting news. The raiders were targeting Hindu households and families. That was the pattern of their carnage. They of course looted Muslim homes too, but on the whole left them alive. But any Muslim suspected of harbouring Hindus or helping them were tortured and killed. Dulhan Begum looked at her daughter in horror even as a thought struck her.

"Your brother's friend on Exchange Road? That is a large Hindu family and will be an easy target for these monsters."

"Their son too is in the militia. Perhaps he has taken the family to safety."

"How could he have done that? He could not have come home just as your brother hasn't."

"But what are we to do? How can we help?"

Dulhan Begum thought for a moment. Her youngest son would be devastated if any misfortune befell his friend and his family. Dulhan Begum thought of the number of evenings that he had spent with that family, enjoying the warmth of friendship and the grace of hospitality that knew no religion. She looked out of the window and looked at the beautiful chinar leaves turning into subdued yellows and then into a glorious orange, against the backdrop of an achingly beautiful blue sky.

How could life be so beautiful yet so horrifying? How could nature's beauty be a witness to the depths of human degradation? How could God not come down to save his people?"

Dulhan Begum thought even as the comforting call of the *azaan* wafted through the garden. She finally turned to her family and said—"Ask Naseer's friend's family to come and stay with us till this disaster is over."

Silence greeted this announcement and then pandemonium broke loose. Dulhan Begum's elderly sister-in-law was the first to speak. "Have you taken leave of your senses Dulhan? You know the consequences of harbouring a Hindu family, or don't you?"

"Chachijaan, this is literally inviting the raiders to come and kill us."

"How will we all fit into this house, even if this was a good idea?"

"Dulhan, you singularly will be responsible for the destruction of this family. Agreed you want to be generous, but not at the cost of your own family."

"I am not going to stay here to be a sitting target for the raiders. I will be safer in Qazikund."

"When the whole family is destroyed and all our daughters abducted what are you going to answer to your sons? Assuming that you are going to be alive to answer them?"

"Do you think the Hindus will be safe with us? They too will be killed. Allah!"

Dulhan Begum waited till everyone had expended their energy shouting.

"I have always been taught that to help somebody, one need not ask permission from practicality. If so nobody will help anybody. I will never be able to face my son if anything happened to that family without me doing anything to help. For a mother, there can be no worse fate. I would like to protect all the Hindu families in Srinagar and in Kashmir. But I can only do as much Allah has given me the means."

"And if in the bargain, we all get killed?"

"If that is what Allah has ordained for us, then how can we ever escape that fate?"

†

The family trooped away, angry and puzzled at Dulhan Begum's adamant stand. Some left the house to hopefully safer havens. Some stayed on, hoping for a change of heart and a retracting of decisions.

Dulhan Begum's daughter looked at her and asked softly— "Ammijan, are you taking this risk as otherwise you will not be able to face Naseer?"

"I am taking this risk, otherwise I will not be able to face my God."

Late into the night Dulhan Begum supervised the cleaning of the rooms and making space for the thirteen guests who would arrive the next day. She created a special kitchen for the Hindu Pundit family since the older orthodox women would not eat food cooked by Muslims. But there was no rancour on this taboo. It was just accepted as a way of life. The next morning, a line of frightened women and children came to Dulhan Begum's home. She stood at the doorway, hands folded in a *namaste*. There were the very old, the not so old, young wives and perplexed children. The men had stayed back to protect the property. Both families faced each other, as Dulhan Begum's daughters helped everyone to find a seat in a crowded *baithak*. Dulhan Begum looked at the children who were scared yet curious at the new turn of events. She whispered to a woman who immediately brought glasses of steaming sugared milk for the children. This familiar childhood routine, immediately soothed the apprehensive children. It sent a reassuring message to the visitors that no matter what the crisis, the familiar routine of a household would carry on reassuringly.

The Hindu guests stayed in the Muslim household for a few days till the disaster blew over. The Indian army arrived just in time to push the raiders back. Kashmir was for the moment safe. Dulhan Begum had every reason to feel happy. Her decision in the face of stiff opposition, resentment and criticism had not jeopardized her family.

In the course of her life, Dulhan Begum faced many a crisis, big and small and each demanded of her a courage that had to be exceptional. Her youngest son studying to be a doctor, falsely accused of spying against Pakistan was imprisoned in the prison at Rawalpindi. The mother in her wept uncontrollably but the woman in her steeled herself for a long fight across unfriendly borders. Her elder daughter took on the task of writing the petitions, meeting people in the corridors of power, arguing, pleading, gathering evidence to support their claim of innocence. Dulhan Begum accompanied her everywhere, hoping that the mother's heartrending plea would find the right response. The

Indian government was sympathetic, but the government in Pakistan was convinced that they had a watertight case against the young medical student. Every night Dulhan Begum would lie awake imagining her son in a small airless cell. She wept thinking of her handsome, suave and fastidious son wearing oversized prison clothes in the filthy conditions of incarceration. But every morning she would get up with a grim determination to get her son freed.

Finally, the Pakistan government handicapped by the fact that there was no irrefutable evidence against Dulhan Begum's son and pressurised by the Indian government, finally agreed for an exchange of prisoners. Dulhan Begum's son was exchanged for a Pakistan army officer captured in 1947. He came home one November morning to Dulhan Begum's arms that had ached for so many months to hold him.

Her youngest son soon became a successful doctor. He was popular and hugely admired. Among the Kashmiri Muslims, he was much sought after, particularly by families with marriageable daughters. Dulhan Begum was human enough to enjoy the attention she got as the mother of a doctor. She was also hugely proud of her educated and successful daughters and sons. Her doctor son went abroad for further studies, enhancing his professional and social status. One day he came home to tell Dulhan Begum that in England, at a civil ceremony, he had married a Kashmiri Pundit doctor. Dulhan Begum was caught in a dilemma. On the one hand, she could see her son was deliriously happy. But she was also apprehensive on the acceptability of an inter religion union in the Kashmiri society. She knew that she could convince her family. But what about the bride's family? Kashmiri Pundits were orthodox and could be very insular. Despite being married the couple were staying in their respective parental homes, waiting for the union to be accepted by both families.

"It will not be easy for a Hindu family to accept a Muslim groom. And that too for their daughter who is a doctor," Dulhan Begum agonised as she sat with her daughters.

"But nobody has a choice. The marriage has taken place. We just have to accept it."

"He says that till both families don't accept it, they will not live together."

"That is easier said than done."

"I know my son and I know the excellent family that his bride comes from. Once they have given their word they will never ever go back on it."

"Do you have a problem with him marrying a Hindu girl?" her daughter asked her point blank.

Dulhan Begum thought for a moment and answered slowly—"I want my son to be happy. I also know that his choice is excellent. She is a lovely person, comes from such an illustrious family, known for their intellect and public service throughout Kashmir. I could not have asked for a better bride. Religious differences have been created by us. So that can and never should be the reason of non-acceptance. But…I want them to be happy. If society does not accept the relationship and her family does not, that will be hugely traumatic for them. I don't want my son to be unhappy. He has had more than his share of anguish."

Tears rolled down Dulhan Begums cheeks.

†

In the Kashmiri society, Hindus and Muslims lived together in perfect amity, but spaces were demarcated. The communities did not dine together in the public spaces, and inter religion unions were few and far between and were frowned upon. In some cases, the 'erring' couples had to leave Kashmir and relocate elsewhere leaving their families to face the social indignity. Dulhan Begum did not want to lose her son to another city or country. She was acutely aware that her daughter-in-law's family was still unbending. She could not just sit and let things take its course. In fact, everything was at a standstill, till one day Dulhan Begum went to her daughter-in-law's family home in Safa Kadal.

The family was stunned to see her at the doorstep. Inherent good manners took over their shock, and they escorted her to the big lounge. The room was huge, reflecting good taste and pride in the Indian and Hindu heritage. Dulhan Begum looked around, as the members of the family made small talk, each skirting the main issue. Soon the bride's mother walked in and folded her hands in a graceful *namaste.* Dulhan Begum held the folded hands in her hands and bowed her head down. For a moment time stood still as two mothers communicated wordlessly their love for their children and the terrible burden that society and its customs was weighing on them.

Dulhan Begum looked at the mother in front of her and said softly—"Behenji, I have four sons. Please take my youngest son into your home and make him a Hindu. I will be the happiest mother."

Dulhan Begum spoke softly, but her voice resonated with the generosity of true motherhood, and the grace of true humanity, unfettered by religious considerations or narrow social norms. Within a few days, word was sent to her son to take his bride home. Dulhan Begum organised a huge and lavish reception to welcome her daughter-in-law. It was her way of telling the world that she was proud of her accomplished daughter-in-law and of her son's decision. The world took their cue from Dulhan Begum and the couple were much welcomed, feted and admired.

A few days later, Dulhan Begum called her son and made him sit next to her. While she held his hands, she said—"Beta, I am proud of you and even more proud of your wife. I truly feel you could not have taken a better decision. But for your wife, brought up in a Hindu home, it will be difficult to adjust in a typical Muslim home. I will look for another house for you. Make that your home and let it reflect the combined culture. We are there for you always as you will be for us."

Her son looked deeply into those generous eyes and kissed Dulhan Begum's hands with reverence because he knew that it was always easy to be a social being. But it took immense courage to be truly human.

The Reluctant Revolt

Madhu

"Madhu, give me another cup of tea." Her husband's voice reached her in the kitchen just as she hurriedly packed the lunch box for the children. She quickly put the kettle to boil and rushed through the process of making tea, even as her son hopped about in impatience.

"Mummy we will surely miss the school bus."

Madhu rushed out, just stopping to grab her dupatta from the chair. As she closed the door she could her husband saying, "Terrible tea".

That morning Madhu caught the chartered bus just in time. As the Assistant Manager of a bank, she could not afford to be late. Particularly now that they had to punch their entry and exit as per the new rules. She heaved a sigh of relief as she sank into the seat next to a well turned out lady. Madhu had always noticed her in the bus. She always looked calm, with not a hair out of place. The woman in Madhu admired her clothes and her jewellery that was always colour coordinated.

Madhu wondered how she had the time to coordinate her clothes and accessories. She barely got time to bathe and change before rushing, thought Madhu as she sighed and took out the rolled rotis that was her breakfast. The smell of the pickle must have wafted to the lady sitting next to Madhu, as she looked up from the newspaper editorial. Madhu smiled apologetically and said "I haven't had breakfast. I hope I am not disturbing you."

"Not at all. You need a good breakfast to last through the day," her eyes twinkled as she reassured Madhu, which emboldened the latter to volunteer more information.

"The mornings are so rushed, that I don't get time to have breakfast."

"Do you get up very late, that you have to rush through the morning?" the lady asked curiously.

"Oh no. I get up at five every morning"

"At five" she ejaculated in surprise. "And yet you have to run to catch the bus at nine?

"Oh I have to get through a lot of housework. I have to cook everyone's breakfast, cook lunch and pack tiffins, wash the clothes and put them out for drying, clean the house, make the beds, get the children ready for school, drop them to the bus stop, pick up the milk on the way back and oh, also make so many cups of tea for my husband." Madhu counted all her chores on her fingers. "I often don't get time to dust the furniture" she sighed. "Doing all this, sometimes, no most times, I don't get time to eat breakfast. But I manage to eat it in the bus." Madhu concluded happily. The lady looked at her and wondered at the complete lack of frustration in Madhu's voice. If at all her voice only reflected a sense of reconciliation at the double duty of a middle class working woman.

†

Madhu had never stopped to wonder at the pace of her daily life. She just accepted it as a given fact in a working woman's life. She was not really unhappy. But she was not really happy either. It was not as if her husband Ramesh ill-treated her. But he didn't treat her well either. Madhu was grateful that he 'permitted' her to work in the bank.

"Let her earn her 'lipstick' money", he would often say patronisingly. It was another thing that the 'lipstick' money Madhu earned was paying off the down payment for the flat they had booked in the suburbs of Delhi. In a small three-bedroom flat occupied by her mother-in-law, unmarried brother-in-law, husband and two children, there was bound to be a lot of work, Madhu reasoned to herself. But sometimes she did feel that she was doing all the chores while the other adults just read newspapers, or watched television, or slept. At such times, Madhu would remember other working women she knew, who shouldered a greater burden of work, and yet were humiliated and taunted.

At least Ramesh is not cruel to me, Madhu thought with gratitude. In any case if she didn't do the chores who would? Madhu accommodated, adjusted and reconciled. That was a middle class woman's life as she saw it.

Next morning, Madhu again sat next to the lady, as on many other days. She liked her and found her easy to talk to. More importantly, she seemed genuinely interested in Madhu's mundane life. In her mind she named the lady 'heroine' as she had only seen heroines in the films wearing such colour coordinated and accessory coordinated outfits. The heroine smiled and asked her mischievously, "Isn't it time to eat your breakfast?"

Madhu smiled sheepishly as she took out her rolled rotis.

"Why don't you do some of your household chores in the evening, so that your mornings are less rushed?"

"Oh I can't do that" said Madhu through mouthfuls. "When I go home, I have to bathe the children, help them with their homework, iron clothes for the next day, cook dinner, serve it and wash up. As it is, I am just able to fit all this in, only because I chop all the vegetables on my way back home in the bus." Madhu was happy to share details of her life.

"Don't you think you are doing too much?"

"Yes, sometimes, but who else will do it? After all taking care of the home is a woman's job isn't it?"

"But you are also earning for the home!"

"Yes, but that is my wish. And to fulfill my wish, I can't neglect my duty as a housewife."

"Tell me Madhu, what do you do with the money that you earn?"

"Oh, my entire salary goes straight towards the payment for the flat we have booked. A four-bedroom flat", she said proudly.

"Oh so your personal wish to earn money is actually building the assets of your family. An asset that your husband too will enjoy."

"Yes" said Madhu slowly wondering where all this was leading to.

"Because of your job, the family is going to benefit. Don't you think that the family should then shoulder some of the household chores in return?"

"Who will do the jobs? How and what will they manage?"

†

The questions rankled in Madhu's mind the whole day in the bank. By evening she dismissed the questions as meaningless, since they could throw up no answers. But that evening as she rolled out the rotis for the family, she could hear them discussing and laughing at the idiosyncrasies of a distant uncle. Nobody included her in the conversation as she walked to and fro between the kitchen and the table to hand out *roti*s hot from the griddle. Her husband and mother-in-law could not eat cold *roti*s. Finally when Madhu sat down to have her dinner, everybody drifted away to watch their favourite show on television. Tears pricked her eyes as she sat silently eating. Was the heroine right? Was she doing so much in the house, that no one else had anything to do? The questions were back to rattle in Madhu's mind. It was past eleven when Madhu came to bed. She had waited till she could hear her husband snoring. She was in no mood for his clumsy lovemaking. But sleep eluded her. In her mind she kept playing all the chores she did and corresponding leisure that everyone else seemed to be enjoying. But that was what she was 'supposed' to do. If she was to fulfill her responsibilities, she needed to finish all her chores. It is all very well for the heroine to ask such questions. She was probably one of those women, who didn't take care of their homes. Or she probably had lots of house help.

But next morning, Madhu again sat next to her and immediately shot out the question paramount in her mind.

"What did you mean when you said I was doing too much work?"

"Madhu I don't have to tell you that. You tell me what it means when even after waking up at five, you need to gobble your breakfast in the bus? That after working whole day in the bank, you need to chop vegetables in the bus before reaching home?"

"It means I don't have time for anything else apart from house work."

"When was the last time you went out for a stroll in the evening or visited a friend or went out for an ice cream, or just sat and lounged in front of the TV or read a book?"

Madhu's silence was answer enough.

"Madhu, you need to work not slog. You treat yourself badly, then why blame the world if they treat you like an unpaid ser vant?"

"But what do I do?"

Madhu had to wait till next morning for the answers

"You need to stop doing the chores that others can do as well."

"Like what?"

"You said that you take the children to the bus stop and bring milk on the way back. Don't bring the milk, since it means a detour for you."

But the children will get no milk the next day and there will…."

"Nobody will fall ill because they did not drink milk for a day."

Next day with a thudding heart, Madhu came back empty handed from the bus stop. When her husband asked for another cup of tea, she said hesitatingly—

"I could not get the milk. I was getting late."

"How can you be so careless Madhu?" her husband spat out in irritation. That was really a mistake on Ramesh's part. If he had kept quiet, Madhu would have repented her small rebellion and rushed out for the milk. But his exasperation provoked her to say—"Why don't you get the milk tomorrow and drop the children to the bus stop? That will give me more time for housework."

The second part of her response was an afterthought to assuage Ramesh's irritation. The next morning Madhu waited expectantly, keeping one eye on the clock to see if Ramesh would get up to drop the children to the bus stop. To her immense relief, he did, even as his mother tried to stop him saying, "Beta you need to read the newspaper. Madhu will drop the children."

"No Ma, I will do it. It is a good exercise for me in the mornings. And I will get the milk too." He ruined the effect of his magnanimity with his next response

"Mind you I will get the milk only on the days the children have school. On holidays Madhu will get it."

Madhu replied from the kitchen—

"On Fridays get extra milk and store it in the fridge." She giggled to herself on her small victory.

Madhu waited expectantly to share her victory with the heroine, who listened with unabashed interest. Madhu was eager for more suggestions.

"Madhu enjoy this victory for some time. You have won only a skirmish, not the war not even the battle."

Madhu was disappointed, but she bided her time.

A few days later, Madhu did not get up early enough to pack her brother-in-law's lunch. He needed to leave home at six to catch the factory bus. Her mother-in-law was furious.

"Why don't you sleep a little less, Madhu, so that you can get up in time?"

"But Ma if I don't get sleep I will fall asleep in the bank. I will lose my job."

"What earthly use is your job anyway to us?"

"I will not be able to buy my lipsticks. And of course pay the instalments," she added. Madhu was surprised at herself. It was as if her small victories were instigating her further. Her brother-in-law started having lunch at the factory canteen.

When Madhu stopped washing the clothes, all hell broke loose. Her mother-in-law taunted her no end on her laziness. Ramesh asked her exasperated— "Madhu, why are you being so slack in your work?"

Madhu looked at him for a minute and said dispassionately—

"I get up in the mornings, bathe the children, get them ready for school, cook breakfast, pack lunches, clean and dust the house, make the beds and then get dressed, travel in a bus and do a whole day's work at the bank. You take the children to the bus stop, get the milk, get dressed and go to work. Your mother gets dressed and lounges in front of the TV. Who exactly are the slack people in this house Ramesh?"

Ramesh looked in disbelief at Madhu. Never before had she taken this stance in all the twelve years of their marriage. He wondered if anything was wrong with her. He could not understand as to why she was making a big deal about the house work. After all women were supposed to do the household chores That was their job. Nevertheless that weekend Ramesh went and bought a washing machine.

†

To Madhu the bus chats were a lifeline. She often wondered if she was doing the right thing. There was an atmosphere of stress in the house all the time. Her mother-in-law was sulky and her husband was grumpy. Was it worth disturbing the peace and happiness of the house?

"What peace are you talking about, Madhu?" asked the heroine. "Everybody else was happy at your expense. And if the family pitches in to help, where is the cause of unhappiness? You have encouraged them to be lazy by taking on every chore. It will take them some time to adjust."

Madhu was always inspired by the heroine's advice. She was sure she could not have ventured on this path of revolt without the support of her heroine.

Things were changing in Madhu's house. A domestic help came in the mornings to help with the cleaning, dusting and washing up. In the mornings Madhu cooked, and got dressed in well matched outfits, and ate breakfast on the table with her husband. The final instalment for the flat had been paid and her husband was going to take possession of the house that week. Madhu waited expectantly for him to invite her to accompany him. After all, she had paid every single instalment. The night before the house was to be handed over, Madhu asked her husband—

"Ramesh shall I accompany you tomorrow?"

"What for? What will you do there? Now it is just the formality of taking possession of the house and getting it registered."

Madhu was stunned for a moment as she comprehended the extent to which her husband had taken her for granted. Slowly and firmly she said—

"I am coming tomorrow Ramesh. I have worked hard at the bank to pay off every instalment. Because my salary paid off the instalment, it did not impact our standard of living."

"So?" Ramesh responded belligerently. "Am I supposed to fall at your feet in gratitude?"

Madhu felt a blinding wave of rage, which she suppressed and said—

"No I don't want you to do that. But the flat will be registered in both our names."

Ramesh stared at her in shock. "And if I don't do that?" he shot back.

"I am coming tomorrow to the developer's office. All payments were made by cheque from my salary account. Ramesh you are intelligent enough to understand what it means. I am not asking it to be registered in my name but in both our names. I for one will not treat you like you don't exist."

†

After the flat was registered in Madhu's and Ramesh's names, she once again sat next to the heroine. From her bag Madhu shyly took out a box and answered mischievously—

"No it is not my breakfast. These are the *mithai*. Yesterday the flat was registered jointly in my and my husband's names."

"Wow Madhu, that is indeed good news. More so that you have the title on the ownership. How did this happen?"

Madhu was only too glad to give the details. "I could not have done all this without you," she said gratefully.

"No Madhu. I just showed you an alternative path. You had the courage to walk on it yourself. You asserted yourself, without any advice from me."

A few days later the heroine stopped travelling in the bus as she had shifted home. Madhu realised that she had never asked her name. In her mind she remained as 'the heroine.'

Sometimes to remind herself of the old Madhu, she eats her breakfast in the car as she is driven to work now.

The Informer

Nusrat Begum

Nusrat Begum watched from a distance as the men lowered the body of her third son into his grave. She said a prayer silently as they threw mud to fill the grave. But the prayer was half-hearted. She was still trying to come to terms with the death of her three sons. All three had taken up arms in the village of Dewar Lolab, fighting for what they thought was the cause of *azadi*. But Nusrat Begum suspected that it was an easy route to quick money. It was difficult to eke out a living from the tiny plot of land which gave only a few quintals of maize. With wives and children to feed, she knew it was difficult life for her strapping sons.

"Curse the ill wind that is blowing over Kashmir. It has destroyed our peace and snatched away our futures," she thought to herself as she comforted her granddaughter. On her way downhill, Nusrat thought of the perverse ways of fate. Her three sons had joined the Hizb ul Mujahideen, the organisation that used terror and targeted killings to achieve the end which was ostensibly 'freedom' for Kashmir. The two elder sons had been killed within a span of two years. The security forces had hunted them down like rats and exterminated them brutally.

"Perhaps my sons too have killed some innocents brutally. Allah can never be unjust," Nusrat thought to herself trying to bring some sense to the senseless killings that surrounded their lives. "But why was Rafiq killed? He was helping the security forces. Why could they not protect him?" Questions rattled in her unquiet mind, as the family made their way home silently.

She entered her small home and the sight of three widowed daughters-in-law grieving silently wrung her heart. Her granddaughters crowded around her trying to get comfort from her presence. She hugged them tight as tears coursed down her cheeks. She cried for the sons who had no more a future. She cried more for her granddaughters who too had no future. How was she to keep Rafiq's family safe? How would she feed them? Her newly widowed daughter-in-law was still young. Would she be safe?

Her head ached as the questions relentlessly repeated themselves. Her elder daughters-in-law were living with their natal families and visited Nusrat Begum infrequently. Rafiq, his wife Shah Begum and their three children lived with Nusrat Begum in the tiny village in Kupwara, tilling the same plot of land that had been in the family for the last three generations. Once the land was enough to feed the entire family of three sons. But with each son claiming his share, the plots became even more fragmented till the land could feed no one fully. But for Nusrat Begum moving away was not even an option. For her this was the security of her family, her home and her refuge. Even when her two sons were killed by the security forces, she clung to the land and the small house. This was the only place she knew in an increasingly uncertain world of bloodshed and death. She knew every apple tree, every little fertile patch. She knew which trees had the sweetest walnuts and which plot gave the best yield of maize.

†

"My brothers-in-law were killed by the security forces for being militants. My husband was killed by militants for helping the security forces. We are caught between two devils. Allah where will I go? What will happen to my children?" Shah Begum wailed inconsolably.

"Why did Rafiq go and become an informer for the army? That is what got him killed." Jabeena her sister-in-law said dispassionately.

"He became an informer, because as a guide for the militants, he was under constant suspicion."

"Why did he have to become a guide for the militants at all?"

"He had to because ever since your husbands turned into militants, the army has not left us in peace. Every day they came and questioned Rafiq. He could not work in peace on the land, nor could he migrate to Srinagar for better work. So what was he to do? Why didn't you ask your husbands the reason why they became militants, putting the entire family at risk?"

Shah Begum was shaking with helpless rage as she lashed out at her sisters-in-law.

"Stop bickering, useless women." Nusrat Begum raised her voice. "Is this the time and place to quarrel, frightening the children! Think about the future."

"It will be dark soon. I need to reach Sopore before night." Jabeena got up, clearly indicating that she was not keen to help

Rafiq's family. Nusrat Begum looked at her elder daughter-in-law in disbelief. When her elder son had been killed the family had rallied around his widow trying to help as much as their meagre means would allow. She looked at her second daughter-in-law who deliberately avoided looking at her. Nusrat Begum had never felt more alone before.

That night, as Nusrat Begum went to the small shed to feed the cow, a tall bearded figure emerged silently from the shadows. Her heart jumped, but she soon recognised him as Shabbir, the local teacher's son who had joined the ranks of militants.

"Khala, you saw what comes out of helping the security forces. Your son was a bastard traitor to the cause. That got him killed."

"He would have been killed even when he was guiding you devils through the mountain pass so that you could wreak havoc on Kashmir. He could have been killed many months before, when he was an informer to the forces. The day he joined you devils his death was certain. Just as yours is."

Shabbir looked perturbed for a moment and he almost looked the naughty boy that Nusrat knew, years ago. But he quickly switched over to his fearful face.

"I have no time to chat with you. I just came to warn you that you should keep away from the security forces or the rest of your family will be killed too." Shabbir disappeared as silently as he had appeared.

†

From that day onwards, there were unwelcome visitors to Nusrat Begum's house. The security forces came to give some money to the family of the informer. But soon the platoon moved away. The relieving platoon felt no responsibility for the family of an information source who was no longer alive.

The militants came regularly under cover of darkness, wanting to know the reasons for the visits of the security forces. This became a pattern. The men wielding guns came, threatening and belligerent, frightening the children till they blubbered in fear. During the time when Rafiq had been an informer for the army, the family had been staying near the army encampment. The militants were trying to ferret information about the layout of the camp from Shah Begum. Often, they looked at Shah Begum who was still comely, despite being a mother to three children. One of them held her hand and said in beguiling tones, "Why don't you come to the forest tomorrow. We need to give you some money. After all, before becoming an informer, your husband has served us well as a guide. Under his guidance, we never ever encountered an army patrol while we were crossing the pass." Shah Begum for a moment looked hopeful, remembering the empty grain bin. But soon she read the underlying meaning as she jerked her hand away in disgust.

The dreaded visits of the militants continued. Sometimes they grabbed the small quantity of food, sometimes they just enjoyed the pleasure of the dread they evoked. Nusrat Begum realised that they were using her house as a shelter at night while keeping a lookout for the security forces as their companions sneaked deeper into the Kupwara area. She knew that it was only a matter of time before the security forces suspected her home and branded them as informers to the militants. Nusrat Begum knew her family was caught irrevocably between two forces, both pitiless and both brutal when suspicious. She also knew that her grandchildren had a future that was bleaker than hell and her daughter-in-law would end up forcibly married to a militant and widowed a second time over. She sat under the apple tree looking at the calm blue sky. Would Allah never see their misery? Would He never protect them? Would He penalise innocent children for the sins of their fathers?

The next morning, Nusrat Begum sold her cow to the local *lambardar.* She knew that he was cheating her. But she was desperate for money. Back home she took out a small paper containing the name of a shelter home for conflict affected women and children in Tangmarg, Baramulla district. A few months earlier before Rafiq had been killed, the supervisor from the home had come to Dewarlolab, to identify women and children in need of shelter. It was sheer chance that Nusrat Begum had picked up the yellow coloured leaflet and kept it in her tattered box. It came in handy now, that her family needed a shelter for some time away from the village and the militants. She hurried her daughter-in-law through her packing and got the children ready. As she washed their faces and combed their hair, her eyes welled up with tears.

"Will I see these beautiful faces again? Will I feel their soft arms around me? Allah what is this test you are putting me through? It is tearing my heart out!" Despite her tumultuous thoughts Nusrat Begum maintained a calm exterior.

"You children are going for a holiday to a home where there will be plenty to eat."

"What about you Dadijan?"

"I have some work here then I too will come and join you."

"Will the *jehadi*s allow you to come? They will try to kill you," piped up her grandson.

Nusrat Begum's heart cried at the loss of innocence.

"Of course not. I am not afraid of them anymore. I am not afraid of them anymore," she repeated it more for herself than for the children.

She saw them off at the bus stop, and waved desperately till it was out of sight.

She turned and made her way deliberately to the army post two kilometres from the village. She pleaded with the guards and sat at the gate stubbornly waiting for the officer to see her. Finally it was late afternoon when the officer called her inside but not before she was frisked for weapons by a lady officer.

When the army major heard her out he was aghast.

"Why do you want to help us?" he asked her plainly.

"Janab, I have already told you that my son was killed for being an informer for the army. Since then the militants have made our lives miserable. They keep visiting our home eating out of our stores, eyeing my daughter-in-law and frightening my grandchildren. I want my family to have a future. That is possible only when these devils are killed. I can help you to kill them."

The officer was weighing the pros and cons of the old woman's proposal. He was also seeing the feather in the platoon's cap if they could nab the militants. Perhaps there would be a cache of arms to be captured. Perhaps he would get a commendation or even the Shaurya Chakra. His inherent caution took over. "How can I be sure that this is not a trap to get my men killed?"

"Janab, I will be there. If I am betraying your trust, you can kill me then and there. Besides your numbers will be much larger. And you will take every precaution to keep your men safe."

The officer and his men questioned her thoroughly, looking for some sign of betrayal. She answered every barked question stoically, with only the faces of her grandchildren in mind. Finally a plan was hatched. Two days later was a moonless night and Nusrat Begum was sure that the militants would come to find out why she visited the army camp. By experience she had learnt that they knew everything that went on in the village. A code was decided by the officer as a signal for the hidden ambush party. She came back to her empty house, tired but grimly determined to ensure that the militants would pay with their lives for having ruined her family's life.

†

Two days later, sure enough when the village was asleep, the militants came in stealthily.

"You old hag, you go and meet the army behind our backs. Isn't it enough that your son has been killed by us?"

"I went to take some money from them. After all my son gave up his life in helping them."

"Oho where is the money?"

Nusrat Begum slowly rummaged in her *pheran* pockets and brought out a thousand rupees, the remaining money from the sale of the cow.

"Where is your daughter-in-law? Have you hidden her from us? We will ferret her out you know."

"She has gone to attend the death anniversary of my eldest son. She will be back tomorrow." Nusrat Begum volunteered the information, in an effort to allay any suspicions.

"Is this the way you treat guests? Is there no food for us?"

Nusrat Begum had been waiting expectantly for this question and jumped up.

"I will kill a chicken for you. In any case we can't feed it so it might as well feed you."

"Mind you, don't try any tricks or there will be a bullet in your old head."

Nusrat Begum killed a chicken, its squawking resounding in the stillness of the night. She waited till the noise died down. Then she deliberately killed another chicken and another. Three chickens killed. Three times the loud squawking resounded. That was the code for the number of the militants holed up in her home. She hoped that the ambush party was waiting. Else she would have killed her chickens for nothing. She said a quick prayer as she went inside. Only Allah knew if she would survive the night.

"Why old woman, you are very generous tonight. Three chickens for us?"

"I want to make some of it for my grandchildren when they come tomorrow."

"If anything is left over after we eat," the men sniggered.

She went into the kitchen to cook for the unwelcome guests. Her heart was thudding and she kept saying quick prayers.

"Allah if death is to come tonight, let it be quick. But please ensure that these devils too are killed. Please keep my family safe and give them a happy future"

Nusrat Begum stopped as she heard the crunch of boots near her kitchen. She knew that the ambush party was surrounding the house. Almost simultaneously, she heard the staccato sound of the machine gun, as the man watching from the window shouted, "Put out the lights. We are being attacked". There was silence in the darkness as she heard a menacing growl.

"The old hag has betrayed us. Slit her throat."

It was pitch dark. She slid down behind the grain bin hoping that the men would not be able to spot her. There was an exchange of gunfire, and a groan. She hoped that one of them at least was fatally shot. Then came a relentless round of fire from the army. She knew that her home was riddled with bullets. She could hear the army men shouting—

"Come out with your hands up. We are going to torch this house and you will be burnt like chickens."

She knew that the militants would never surrender. To be caught alive was a fate worse than death for them.

How would she escape? If she went out, she would be shot. If she stayed inside she would be burnt alive. Nusrat Begum had to think fast. She slowly crawled to the back door and opened the door slightly. Almost immediately there was a burst of gunfire. She crawled out shouting all the while—

"Don't shoot. I am an old woman." There was silence as she crawled to the shed and sat there shivering. Her hands and knees were grazed and bleeding. "At least I am alive. But for how long?"

Intermittent firing continued throughout the night. By early morning light there was an eerie silence from the house. The bullet proof clad army men cautiously peeped through the windows and found three men sprawled, stone dead in the room. Nusrat Begum watched silently as the bodies were carried out. The village gathered around looking at the ruin that her house had become. Every window was shattered. Bullet holes gaped widely on the walls. In one corner, the wall had collapsed after a grenade burst. The army major drove down to congratulate his men. But he showed no recognition of the chief architect of the ambush. Nusrat Begum was thankful for his sensitivity. In the eyes of the village she was the victim. In any case dead men tell no tales. As the ambush party was driving away, the army major came up to her, ostensibly to question her. He looked at her and said softly, "Cover the chickens. They are good to be cooked".

Nusrat Begum wandered into her home, now charred and blackened, a mute symbol of her family. She looked around dispiritedly and saw every corner that had once resonated with happy laughter. A lifetime of memories was burnt down in the space of a single night. In the kitchen she saw the three birds that she had killed. They had served their purpose. Even the thought of cooking made her sick. As she picked them up to distribute among her neighbours, she saw a small packet. It contained some money that the army major had left behind to help her tide over her immediate crisis. Seeing the money galvanised Nusrat Begum. She knew that she had no time to spare. Word would have spread on the death of the militants. She knew another round of visits would begin to make her pay for the death of the members of the cadre. She quickly packed her small bundle of belongings, and took the bus to Baramulla. As she turned to look at her house, she knew that she had made a break with all that was familiar and known. She was now going into uncharted seas and nothing would be the same. She had pulled out her roots and now she was adrift in the world. It was a big price to pay for her family's safety. But worth it, she thought.

"I must apply for compensation from the army for the damage to my home. But that is another day."The bus trundled away taking Nusrat Begum to a new life.

Acknowledgements

Many of the stories in this collection were inspired by real life incidents. I had the incredible opportunity to hear from and hear of these amazing women who within the constraints of cultural, social and familial straitjackets, fought to discover their courage and assert their personhood. I am immensely grateful for this inspiration.

I acknowledge the perceptive insight of my publishers Niyogi Books, particularly Tultul Niyogi, Nirmalkanti Bhattacharjee and Mohua Mitra, my patient and helpful editor.

Dr. Malashri Lal, my friend and strong sounding board who painstakingly went through the stories with an eagle eye while pre-editing it. Some of these stories were conceived and written while enjoying the gracious hospitality of her home Shyamoli in Jaipur.

Dr. Mohini Giri who gave me the opportunity to volunteer with the Guild. During the course of fulfilling the mandate of empowering under privileged women, I had the opportunity to travel and meet many amazing women.

The late Dr. Girija Dhar who usually was the first reader of these stories since many were written in her beautiful garden in Srinagar.

Amma and Achan, my parents who inspired me to explore the immense challenge of writing creatively.

Medha my daughter who is both a critic and an admirer, and who has truly touching faith in me.

Deven my husband who gave me the tremendous intellectual space and the materially conducive environment to write.

Glossary

Amma: Mother

Annapoorna: The Indian goddess of food

Azaan: The Islamic call to prayer

Ayyagaru: Sir in Telugu

Azadi: Freedom

Baitak: Lounge

Beedi: Type of cheap cigarette made of unprocessed tobacco wrapped in leaf, popular in South Asia

Behen: Sister

Beti: Daughter

Bhai: Brother

Bharta: A dish made with mashed eggplant cooked with Indian spices

Bhoot: Ghost

Burka: A long, loose garment covering the whole body from head to feet, worn in public by many Muslim women

Chacha: Uncle, specifically father's brother

Chachijan: Aunt. Specifically the wife of father's younger brother, the suffix *jan* meaning life and used as a term of endearment

Chaiji: 'Mother' in Punjabi language

Chapattis: A flat coarse unleavened bread resembling a pancake

Chechi: Elder sister in Malayalam language

Chillis: Small green peppers

Chittappa: Uncle in the Tamil language

Dadijan: Father's mother. The suffix *jan* meaning life is term of endearment

Darpoke: Term of derision for frightened people

Dharna: The practice of exacting justice or compliance with a just demand by sitting and fasting at the doorstep of an offender until the demand is granted

Dupatta: Length of material worn as a scarf or head covering, typically with a salwar, by women from South Asia

Fauji: Soldier

Fidayeen: Commando or guerrilla who sacrifices himself

Garu: A respectful form of address in Telugu

Gora: Whiteman. In this context the British officer

Hai Rabba: Dear God

Hai Ram: Dear God

Janab: Honourable/sir/your honour in Urdu

Jehadis: One engaged in jihad, in armed conflict

Jhansi ki Rani: An Indian queen known and admired for her defiance of the British in 1557

Kabalis: The raiders from across the borders in 1947

Kafir: Non believer. Normally used in the context of non Muslim

Kahwa: The traditional green tea preparation consumed in Kashmir Valley

Kaala pani: The British Indian prison on the Andaman and Nicobar Islands was referred to as *kaala pani*. The stretch of ocean between mainland India and the islands was also termed *kaala pani*, crossing it spelt doom

Khala: Aunt in Urdu

Khap Panchayat: A Khap is a community organisation representing a clan or a group of related clans. A Khap Panchayat is an assembly of Khap elders

Kismet: Fate

Lambardar: Village headman

Lathi: a long heavy wooden stick used as a weapon in India, especially by the police

Lingam: A symbol of divine generative energy, especially a phallus or phallic object as a symbol of Shiva

Masi: Aunt

Maulvi: An expert in, or teacher of Islamic law

Mehar: A mandatory amount of money agreed upon at the time of a Muslim marriage, paid by the husband to the wife during a divorce

Mohalla: Neighbourhood

Namaaz: The ritual prayers prescribed by Islam to be observed five times a day

Namaste: Traditional greeting bringing palms together

Panchayat Mukhiya: Head of the panchayat. The Headman

Paranthas: A flat, thick piece of unleavened Indian bread fried on a griddle.

Pheran: A long coat or cloak made of wool or tweed, worn both by women and men in Kashmir

Punditain: A female pundit or the wife of a pundit. Pundit is a Brahmin scholar or a teacher of any field of knowledge in Hinduism, particularly the Vedic scriptures.

Rakhi: North Indian festival when brothers pledge to protect their sisters

Rotis: A flat coarse unleavened bread resembling a pancake

Saheb: Hindi equivalent to 'Sir'

Sarkar: Government

Shabaash: Well done

Shaurya Chakra: An Indian military decoration awarded for valour, courageous action or self-sacrifice while not engaged in direct action with the enemy

Sindoor: Red pigment made from powdered red lead, applied as a dot on the forehead or in the parting of the hair of married Hindu women

Talaq: A form of divorce under Islamic law in which the husband repudiates the marriage by saying 'talaq' three times

Teacher ji: Ji is the suffix added to give respect

Thana: Police station

Tongas: Horse driven carts

Wazir Wazarat: Wazir is a high ranking official in a Muslim government and Wazarat is the Ministry or administration. In this context the Governor of Muzaffarabad

Writer, poet, and social activist **Meera Khanna** is the Trustee and Executive Vice President of the Guild of Service, an NGO working with and for the empowerment of vulnerable women and children.

She has worked as a Consultant on the status of women, Government of India, served as a member on the Expert Committee on Widows constituted by the Supreme Court of India and is on the Global Steering Committee working on a treaty on violence against women. She has helped create a global alliance, 'The Last Woman First.' for empowering under privileged women.

Meera Khanna has written on women's rights for newspapers, journals and collections and her creative expressions have been adapted for dance. She is a published author with a book on career counselling. A collection of poems on Kashmir and her last work based on real life narratives have been widely acclaimed.

Others books with women protagonists from the Niyogi Books stable that you may like to read

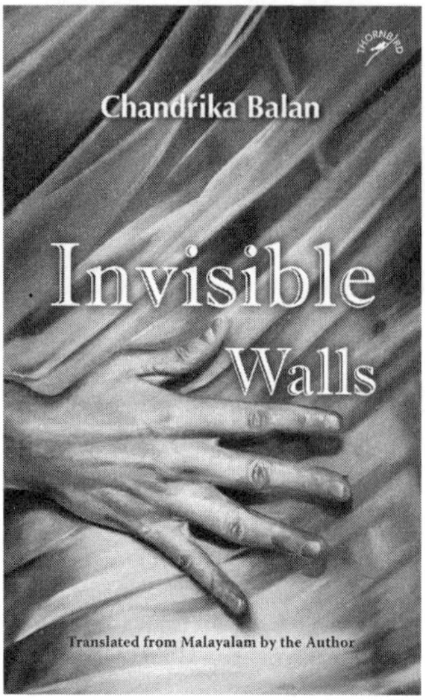

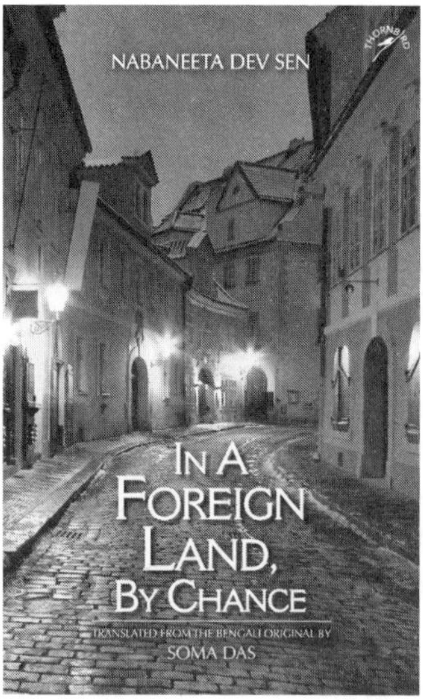